Terrifying Tales

13 Scary Stories for Children

David Kobb   Shawn Kobb

Introduction

This book contains a collection of scary tales that are meant to give you a fright. We love to scare our readers. However, please remember that all the stories in this book are the work of the authors' imaginations.

None of the scary creatures in these tales are real. Bigfoot doesn't exist. There is nothing hiding in your closet.

Turn off the light and climb under the blankets. You can sleep easy, dear readers.

You are safe. I'll see you soon.

- David Kobb

Introduction - Part 2

I want you to know that all of these scary tales are true.

There are monsters in your closet just waiting for you to close your eyes. There are nightmares in the woods and walking the halls of your school. The boogeyman is real.

Don't listen to what David said on the previous page. He's trying to trick you. He wants you to feel safe. He wants you to let your guard down. Don't fall for it. That's how they get you.

Sometimes the noises you hear at night aren't just your imagination.

Sweet dreams...

- Shawn Kobb

Ol' Baldy

By Shawn Kobb

Derrick's nickel bounced off the top of Ol' Baldy's head with a dull clunk. His family probably had more money than the rest of this miserable town combined. Using nickels instead of pennies like the rest of us was his way of making sure we didn't forget.

"Nailed it!" he said.

"Luck," I said.

"Whatever. Let's see you do it. Got any *pennies* left?"

I'm not sure if he emphasized pennies or I just imagined it.

"That's enough for today," I said. I was out of pennies, but I didn't want him to know that.

We got on our bikes and started back to town. Baldy's Well was just on the edge of town in an overgrown park that the city could no longer keep up. It still got the occasional picnicker, but it mostly attracted bored kids like us who came to flip pennies (or nickels) into the well.

The well was made of old stones covered in moss and had the rotted remains of a wooden post on top that probably once lowered a bucket. Now it served as part wishing well, part ghost story. Every few years some over-protective parent would insist the city fill it in. The town would compromise with some sort of cover and kids would promptly uncover it.

We could see the water about twenty feet down. Nobody knew if it went deeper or if that was the bottom. Since the depth never seemed to change I kind of thought it didn't go any deeper. You could see Ol' Baldy's head down below.

I was nine so I wasn't stupid. The town kids told ghost stories about Ol' Baldy and how he'd sometimes come out of the well and grab an unsuspecting kid, but it was really just a shiny white rock with a bit of moss that looked like hair.

"Jimmy told me just two years ago a kid from Jasper got grabbed by Ol' Baldy," Derrick said.

"Your brother's full of crap," I said. "We'd have heard if that happened."

"Not if the kid was from Jasper," Derrick said, his cheeks flushing as red as his hair. "It might not have been in our news."

"Maybe," I said. "'Course, Ol' Baldy isn't real anyway so that probably means it didn't happen."

"That *rock* might not be Ol' Baldy, but that doesn't mean he ain't real. Maybe he's just down deeper."

It wasn't the first time we had this debate. Derrick liked to freak me out. I hated when we had ghost stories around the fire with our friends because they knew they could scare me. I couldn't seem to stop from getting scared no matter how hard I tried.

"Bull crap," I said. As I'd gotten older I started using more adult language.

Derrick skidded his bike to a stop. "If you know so much why don't we come back tonight and flip pennies?"

"Tonight?"

"After. Dark." Derrick said as he looked straight in my eyes. "Unless you're too chicken..."

"My mom will never let me ride out there after dark. Neither will yours. Lucky for you. Saves you from looking stupid."

"You're just scared," Derrick said. "You tell your mom you're going to my place and I tell my mom I'm going to yours. You know they won't check."

He was right. We'd done it before. We did sleep overs all the time and the parents never called to check. I couldn't think of a good excuse.

"Fine," I said.

"We'll meet in front of my place at 8:30."

I told my parents I was going to Derrick's to play video games later. I hoped my mom would say no. I even tried to give her an out by bringing up the fact we were going to visit my aunt the next day, but it was summer and she didn't mind. I found Derrick waiting in front of his house at the agreed upon time.

The ride to Baldy's Well was a silent one. I was lost in thought. I guess Derrick was too. Normally the park felt a bit wild, overgrown, but after dark it seemed to take on a sinister air. I was disappointed to not find any high-schoolers there making out.

Derrick acted braver and peered over the edge. The moonlight glistened off the top of Ol' Baldy. He flipped a nickel and hit the crown dead on.

"There," he said. "I woke him up. Let's see what happens if you try."

Sweat collected on my upper lip. I knew nothing would happen, but I couldn't help it. I grabbed a penny from my pocket and balanced the coin on my thumbnail. With a flip it was up and falling. I peered over to see where it landed.

"Ahh!"

I screamed and nearly peed my pants when Derrick shouted and fake pushed me like I was going in.

"You butthole!" I yelled as I stumbled a few steps back from the well. I was out of breath and trying hard not to shake.

Derrick doubled over laughing. At that moment I wanted nothing more than to punch him right in the mouth.

"You should have seen your face," he said. "It was hysterical!"

It was behind him so he couldn't see it and my mouth opened, but I couldn't make any sound come out. A shiny white dome, the top covered in something damp, stringy, and brown crept above the edge of the well. Two black holes that should have held eyes, but instead were only full of wriggling worms looked at me, and then turned their slimy gaze toward Derrick.

He screamed as boney fingers grabbed his wrist and yanked him over the edge of the well. I heard a splash, the water sounding deeper than I ever would have thought.

I couldn't breathe. I yelled Derrick's name. I yelled for my mom. Mostly I just made sounds of pure terror.

I knew I had to help. I wanted to get out of there, but forced myself to run back to the side of the well. I peeked over the side and looked down into the darkness.

The pale, ghostly light of the full moon shone on the bottom of the well. The water was perfectly still, broken only by the top of Ol' Baldy's head and a smaller dome next to it, bits of bright orange hair on top just visible in the moonlight.

Death Rides a Bike

By David Kobb

Sam sprawled across the couch enjoying another beautiful summer day spent inside playing video games. Much to his mother's frustration, he didn't like going outside much. Even during summer break when all of his friends were out skating or playing basketball, he liked staying inside. He was happy doing as little as possible. His mom, however, did not approve of what she called his *lazy dog* ways.

"Sammy, you're not spending another beautiful day inside. You're twelve years old. You should be out playing with your friends. Don't you want to enjoy your summer break?"

Sam paused his game and looked at his mom, trying hard not to roll his eyes. "I'm happy right now. Why do I need to go outside?"

"It's not healthy to spend all your time indoors. You need exercise."

Sam grunted his contempt for exercise.

"You need to spend some time in the sun," his mother continued. "You're so pale."

"The sun gives people cancer," Sam said, a note of condescension in his voice.

"Video games give people cancer," his mom said with a huff.

"What?" Sam exclaimed. "Cite your sources!"

His mom moved toward the video game system, and Sam began to panic.

"What are you doing mom?" he asked nervously.

"You're going outside," she said, reaching toward the power button.

"Wait! Wait!"

She ignored his protests.

"At *least* let me save it," he begged.

His pleas were too late. She pushed the power button until the green light turned red. His hours of hard work were gone in an instant. He put his head in his hands and sighed.

"You have a brand new bike in the garage, and you've barely touched it."

"I told you I didn't *want* a bike for my birthday. I wanted Smash and Dash Dynasty," he said, mentioning the game he wanted for his birthday but didn't get.

"Well you got a bike. A lot of kids would love to have a new bike."

"Then give it to *them*," Sam said with a grumble.

His mother moved to stand in front of him. She pointed toward the garage. "Out," she said. "Get on your bike and go. Don't come back until sundown. I can't believe I have to force you to go have fun."

Sam stood and stomped away from his mom and toward the front door. "I was having fun!" he said.

His mother yelled at his back as he left the house, "And wear your helmet!"

Sam grabbed his bike out of the garage, made a point to leave his helmet where it was, and rode down the driveway.

As he rode down the street Sam admitted that the day *was* pretty nice. He thought about riding to his friend Micah's house. Micah had the best video games, and most of them were two player, but then he remembered that Micah was away out of town for the summer, visiting his grandma. He decided just to ride around town and see where he ended up.

Sam turned off of Main Street and on to Willow Avenue. He rode on the sidewalk near the houses and yards. He was beginning to actually enjoy himself when suddenly a monstrous German Shepard leapt against the fence he was riding near. The dog slobbered and snarled, woofing at him in a demonic howl. Sam sped up and rushed away from the beast.

He looked over his shoulder at the still crazed dog, and when he looked back his eyes widened. He had ridden into the middle of an intersection without realizing it. At the same time Sam entered the intersection a red minivan blew through a stop sign. He felt the wind from the van rush across his face as it kept driving. It didn't even slow down. Sam had hit the brakes so hard that the back tire of his bike came off the ground and he nearly flipped over the handle bars.

"Holy cow!" Sam exclaimed, "That was close."

He did a quick check to make sure he was okay, patting himself on the arms, head and chest. His heart raced, but otherwise, he seemed to be in one piece. This is what happens when you go outside, he thought. He'd have to remember to tell his mom. That would show her.

As he peddled on, Sam felt watched. He looked around at the houses he passed but didn't see anyone. Still, the feeling continued. By some instinct, he looked over his shoulder. There, in the distance, was another bike rider. The rider was too far way for Sam to make out any details. Just another kid out for a ride, Sam decided, and he kept going.

Sam still didn't know where he was heading, or what he wanted to do. He considered riding down to the skate park. Some of his friends liked to hang out there even though they weren't good skaters. Mostly they just sat on their boards and talked. The older kids who could actually skate hated Sam and his friends getting in the way. Some of those kids were actually pretty scary, so he decided against going.

He turned off of Willow and onto Roosevelt. The houses on Roosevelt were large and old, the same kind of houses that were always haunted in scary movies. They loomed over the road like menacing birds, like black crows on a power line. A shiver ran down Sam's spine.

Something made him look over his shoulder. He couldn't explain the feeling, but a nagging voice in his head urged him to look. There, closer than before but still in the distance, the other rider was still following him. Sam couldn't see the person very well, but he made out a little more detail than before. What he saw raised the hairs on the back of his neck. The person on the bike, the person that seemed to be following him, wasn't another kid. It was an adult.

Sam thought it could be a coincidence. He figured a lot of people ride their bikes on summer days. He tried to convince himself that the rider wasn't someone to be worried about, just a person enjoying their day. However, as he rode on, he couldn't help thinking that the houses on Roosevelt loomed over him like he was prey, and they looked so very hungry.

He decided to get off of Roosevelt. At the first side street he came across, he turned left. He wasn't sure what road he was on now, but he was off of Roosevelt and that was all that mattered at that moment. A little part of him did wonder if that other bike rider was going to follow him, but he forced himself not to care. He wouldn't look back.

As he rode on the old saying *out of the frying pan and into the fire* entered Sam's head. Fairview Cemetery stretched as far as the eye could see on the left side of the road, and Elmwood Cemetery stretched into the distance on the right. Sam felt his stomach clench. He couldn't resist any longer, something about the cemeteries made him look over his shoulder.

There, even closer, the rider was behind him. Now, he was only around 100 feet away. He was close enough that Sam could get a better look at the person. It was a man. He was tall and reed-thin and dressed all in black.

Sam's first instinct was to speed away, but he worried the man might just keep following him. Without meaning to, Sam stopped pedaling. He only noticed he was slowing down when he was nearly standing still, and the bike wobbled. He put his feet down to stabilize himself and stood motionless on the side of the road. As he stopped, so too did the other rider.

Sam waited for the other rider to do or say something. He sat uncomfortably on the bike seat and stared. The rider stared back.

Sam noticed that the sun had moved and was now half-hidden behind the elm trees that gave the cemetery on his right its name. In a near panic a thought entered his mind – he had to get home.

Sam turned and pedaled away from the rider. The rider followed. Sam pedaled faster. On his left and right, the many gravestones streaked along his peripheral view. The rider kept pace.

Sam felt like he was racing both the rider and the night, the sun having almost entirely fallen behind the tall elms.

His breath came in short gasps. His legs burned with the unknown effort. Sam checked his shoulder. Still the tall man followed.

Finally the cemeteries ended, and Sam took the first side street left. He raced ahead, pedaling with the energy only fear can provide.

He looked over his shoulder again. The tall man was gaining on him. His skeleton body barely seemed to move, but somehow he was getting catching up.

Sam turned right on the next street, and then immediately turned left onto an alley. He furiously pumped his legs, willing his bike to move faster.

He spared a glance over his shoulder, and still the rider hunted him. Closer. The rider was so close now that Sam could see the brand name of the bike he rode. It was a Scythe.

Sam saw a street intersecting the alley just a little ways away, and there were people walking down the sidewalk. Where there were people, there was safety, he thought. He put forth one last effort on the pedals.

Sam neared the end of the alley going as fast as he ever had on a bike. He flew from the alley, like a gunshot, and passed over the sidewalk, and in a blink he was in the road.

The pizza delivery driver never had a chance to stop. He was going nearly forty miles per hour when he hit Sam.

Sam woke up on the ground, and blinked his head clear. Standing over him was the man that he had been fleeing. He held his long, thin, boney fingers out to Sam. For some reason, Sam's fear of the man was gone. He took the man's hand for assistance and stood up. The man was even taller and thinner than Sam had first suspected. The man's Scythe bike, black and chrome, stood nearby. He motioned for Sam to follow. Sam picked up his bike and rode after the man.

As he rode off, Sam glanced over his shoulder. He saw that there had been an accident. Someone, a boy, had been hit by a pizza delivery car while riding his bike. The boy looked familiar. Never mind, Sam thought. He turned away and followed the tall man, dressed all in black, down the road.

Bring Your Child to Work Day

By David Kobb

It was bring your child to work day.

Jacob got out of bed before his alarm went off. He was dressed and downstairs before his mom was even awake. She came into the kitchen as he poured milk into his bowl of cereal.

"You're up early," she said sounding surprised.

"Going to work with dad today," Jacob explained, his mouth full of half chewed food.

"Swallow and then speak, Jakey. We talked about this. They're called manners. Remember?"

"Mom, please don't call me Jakey. It's just Jake or Jacob now. *Remember*?" he said imitating his mother. "We talked about this."

"Don't sass me. You're thirteen, but I could still put you over my knee." She ruffled his hair to take the sting out of her words.

He heard his dad wake and start to get ready for the day, electric razor buzzing, and then the shower running.

"So, you're going to do exactly what dad tells you to, right?" his mom asked.

"Yeah, sure."

"I mean it Jake. Your dad's job is dangerous and you could get hurt if you don't pay attention to what he says."

"It's not like we live in a dangerous place, mom. It's *Lumpkin,*" he said the name of the town in which they lived as if it provided the best argument against his mother's concerns.

"Even in Lumpkin bad things can happen and bad people can cause trouble."

Jacob's mom poured herself a glass of orange juice and sat at the table across from him. She looked him in the eye. "There are bad people all over the world. In big cities, and even in small towns like ours. You have to keep a good head on your shoulders, or you might lose it entirely."

"I'm not a kid anymore. You have to stop worrying so much."

"I know you're not a kid, but..."

At that moment Jacob's dad came into the kitchen and said, "What's for dinner?"

Jacob's dad loved to say the wrong name for whatever meal he was eating. He'd call lunch breakfast and dinner lunch. For some reason Jacob couldn't understand, his dad always thought it was the funniest thing.

"Whatever you want to make yourself," Jacob's mom said, rolling her eyes.

"Morning, Jakey," his dad said giving him a soft punch on the shoulder. He poured himself a cup of coffee that Jake's mom had just finished making.

"Morning, dad," Jake responded.

"Oh, so he gets to call you Jakey" his mom asked.

"It's different, ma."

"Oh, sure, it's different. You're all grown up now unless dad's around."

"You excited to come to work with me today?" Jake's dad asked, interrupting the argument before it had a chance to really take off.

"Yeah, should be fun. I was thinking you could let me drive the squad car, and maybe we could fire off a few rounds at the range."

"You're not doing either of those. Isn't that right?" Jacob's mom said, staring daggers at his dad.

"Nope. We'll mostly be doing paper work."

"Aw, come on dad," Jake sighed.

"Well, maybe I'll let you interrogate a prisoner. If you're good," Jakes dad said winking at his mom when Jake wasn't looking.

"That'd be awesome! You could be good cop, and I'll be bad cop," Jake said nearly bouncing in his chair.

"Honey," Jake's mom said, frowning at him, "your dad is kidding. You can't be so gullible."

"Aw, leave him alone. He's not gullible. He's trusting," his dad said, coming to his rescue.

"He's too trusting. One day it's going to get him in trouble. He's going to trust the wrong person, and they're going to hurt him."

Jake felt like his mom was always trying to put him down, but he could always count on dad to come to his aid.

"He's a good kid, and he sees the good in other people. Is that so wrong?"

His dad got up from the table, drained the last of his coffee, and adjusted his service belt. "Time to hit the road, kiddo," he said to Jake.

"Wait," Jake's mom said to his dad. "You didn't eat anything."

"Don't worry. There will be doughnuts at the station."

As Jake walked toward the front door, he saw his mom grab his dad's hand and stop him.

"Watch out for him. You will, right? Keep him safe?"

"Honey, of course. Besides, it's *Lumpkin*!"

"Can I drive to us to the station," Jacob asked his dad?

"Nope."

"Why not?"

"You're not old enough and it's illegal. I'd have to call the police," his dad laughed at his own joke.

"When can I drive? At this rate I'm going to grow old and die before you let me drive."

"I promise you, it will be before you die."

Jake's house was on the opposite side of town from the police station. They had to drive all the way across town and it took a whole three minutes.

Lumpkin was one new resident shy of a population of 200 people. Most people that lived in Lumpkin were farmers. They grew soybeans and corn, and they raised livestock. The popular saying was that there are more horses in Lumpkin than people, and there are more sheep than horses, and more cattle than sheep. People talk about one stoplight towns. Lumpkin had one stop *sign*. The most recent criminal excitement in town was when old Mr. Fielder thought someone was stealing his mail. It turned out he just didn't get any.

They pulled up to the police station at the same time Officer Bobby was pulling up. They all got out of their cars at the same time.

"Hey, Bobby," Jake's dad said.

"Morning, Greg," Office Bobby said, waving at Jake's dad. "Morning, Jake."

"Morning, Officer Bobby," Jake responded.

"Ethan didn't come in with you?" Jake's dad asked.

"Nah. He's been sick the last couple of days."

Jake inwardly breathed a sigh of relief. Officer Bobby was a nice guy, but Jake couldn't stand his son. Ethan was in the same grade as Jacob and he was always picking his nose, and Jake even saw him eat a booger once.

"Yeah, he was puking all over last night," Bobby said, shaking his head in disgust.

"Maybe it was something he ate," Jake said.

The three of them walked to the station.

It was a small building, fitting a town the size of Lumpkin. It was made entirely of grey limestone. Jake always thought it looked like one of the mausoleums in the cemetery. The windows had rusting bars on them. The plaque hanging next to the door said the station had been constructed in 1884, and there hadn't been many changes made to it since it then.

At the door, Jake's dad pressed an intercom buzzer. He looked down at Jake and shrugged, "I misplaced my keys a couple of days ago. Haven't bothered getting them replaced yet. Usually, I get buzzed in."

They entered the station and the door locked behind them.

The only other officer in the station was Officer Shelly Lawrence.

They all exchanged greetings, and Officer Lawrence began to talk to his dad about work stuff, which Jake immediately tuned out.

"Brought one in overnight," Officer Lawrence said, motioning toward one of the cells at the back of the room.

"What's he in on?" Jake's dad asked, taking a long look at the sleeping figure in the cell.

The cells in the station were of the old style, with metal bars on three of the sides and a limestone wall on the fourth.

"Trespassing, and no identification."

"How's that?" Bobby asked for clarification.

"Well, Officer Becker got a call from Mrs. O'Grady last night about someone walking through her backyard, so he went to check it out. Found this guy walking along the side of the road by the time he got there. Asked the guy for ID and why he was walking through Mrs. O'Grady's property. Guy says he doesn't have any ID, and that he didn't know he was walking on anyone's property. Says he's just trying to get to the next town. So, Becker asks his name and the guy can't think of one. So, Becker tells him he's got to bring him in, if he doesn't have ID, so that's what he does."

"Fingerprint him?" Bobby asked.

"Oh, yeah. Sure. Only the system's not working again, so we had to send the scanned prints off to Fort Banger, so they could run 'em for us. They should be getting the results back to us anytime now."

"Well, I guess that's that," Bobby said.

"Yeah, boys. That's about it. I'm heading home now."

"Bye, Shelly," Jake's dad said, watching her walk out the door.

"Guess, I'll saddle up, and hit the dusty trail," Bobby said, heading toward the door.

Jake watched Bobby leave, the door locking behind him. Jake and his dad were left all alone in the station. Well, *almost* alone.

The man in the cell coughed and turned over. He still seemed to be asleep. Jake stared at the man. He didn't look like a criminal. He didn't have any scars on his face, or gang tattoos, or any other of the marks television always thought criminals had. He just looked like a regular guy.

The only interesting thing about his appearance was how thin he was.

"Don't talk to him, son," Jake's dad said, seeming to read his mind.

"I wasn't thinking about it," Jake lied.

"He's probably harmless, but it doesn't matter. He's in the cell, and that means he's none of your business."

"It doesn't seem like a person should be arrested just because they walk through someone else's yard. It's not like he hurt anything." Jake finally took his eyes off the man.

"You like to see the best in people, Jake. I admire it. It's a good trait to have. Most likely the fingerprints will come back and the guy will be clean. I'll let him go with a warning when that happens. Sound good?"

"Yeah."

The phone on Jake's dad's desk began to ring.

"Lumpkin police station, what can I do for you?" his dad asked into the phone receiver.

Jake only heard his dad's side of the conversation.

"Yeah? How many shots? How long ago? Address? Okay. I'll get over there as soon as possible."

30

His dad hung up the phone and keyed the radio on his desk.

"Bobby, this is Greg. Just got a call. Neighbors say they heard shots fired at the Knapp residence at 707 Pine."

There was a moment of static and then Bobby responded, "Shots fired? Roger. I'm on my way."

"Shots fired?" Jake asked, his breath coming in shallow gulps.

"That's what the neighbor said." Jake's dad got out of his desk chair, and looked at Jake. "You can't come, so don't even ask."

"But dad..."

"No. Too dangerous. Play around on the internet on my computer, but don't touch anything else." He headed for the door and stopped. "The buzzer for the door is on the wall over there," he said pointing to a large red button set on the wall near the entrance. Buzz me in when I get back."

Jack watched angrily as his dad left. It wasn't fair, he thought. Finally some excitement in Lumpkin and he was left to check Facebook.

Jake was playing a first-person shooter on his dad's computer when he heard someone say his name. He nearly fell out of his chair.

"Hey, Jake."

Jake turned around and saw the man in the cell standing, hands wrapped around the bars.

"I can't talk to you," Jake said, forcing himself to turn back around.

"You just did, Jake."

The man had some sort of accent that Jake couldn't place. He ignored him.

"Listen, I know you are not supposed to talk to me, but your father wouldn't disapprove of this conversation. I have a thirst, Jake. I need some water. Can you bring me some, please?"

Jake turned the volume up on the computer. The sound of shotgun blasts, and growling zombies intensified.

"You were right, you know? A man shouldn't be arrested simply for walking along some grass. Who says anyone has more of a right to piece of land than anyone else? Are we not all equal?"

Jake didn't know what the man was talking about, but even with the computer volume at full blast, he couldn't tune the man out. Something about the way he spoke. Something about his voice. It was like honey in Jake's ears. It was soothing, like the sound of ocean waves lapping on a beach.

"If it will get you to stop talking, I'll get you some water."

"There, I knew you were a good sort. I could tell the moment I first saw you. It's in the eyes, Jake. You have kind eyes."

Jake walked over to the water cooler and filled one of the paper cones with water. He turned to face the cell and froze, suddenly realizing the only way he could give the water to that man was by handing it to him. That meant he'd have to get close to him. Very close.

"What is the matter, son? Just bring it on over," the man persuaded.

Jake drank the water from the cone and threw it in the garbage. He went back to his dad's desk and grabbed a coffee mug. He went back to the water cooler and filled the mug. Then he walked over to the cell, and set the mug on the ground, far from the bars.

"Not going to do me much good there, Jake," the man said, pointing at the mug on the ground.

"Hold on," Jake replied.

Jake walked over to a closet, opened the door and removed a broom and then walked back in front of the cell. He used the broom to push the coffee mug toward the bars until the man bent down and picked up the mug. Jake jerked the broom back quickly, as if there was something the man could have done with the broom if he had grabbed it from Jake.

The man smiled. "I am not a witch. Couldn't fly from here with that broom even if I wanted to." He paused a moment. "You afraid of me, Jake?"

Jake's first instinct was to lie, but for reasons he couldn't understand, it felt wrong to lie to this man. "I am. I am very afraid of you."

"And why are you afraid?"

"You're in the cell. You must have done something wrong."

"Must I have? Are no innocent people ever arrested?"

"Sometimes," Jake admitted.

"Then there is the chance that I am innocent."

"Maybe."

"Well, Jake. As long as we understand each other. Thank you for the water."

The man moved back to the cot at the far side of the cell, and sat. He held the mug but did not drink. He kept his eyes locked onto Jake's until Jake had to turn away.

Jake returned to his father's desk and un-paused the game, but couldn't concentrate. He considered what the man said. Innocent people are arrested often. Even his father said that sometimes innocent people were arrested and that was why there were courts, to figure out who was guilty and who was innocent. Isn't it possible that this man didn't mean any harm by walking through Mrs. O'Grady's property? Jake himself had often moved through property that wasn't owned by his family. He played hide and go seek in the summer and used the entire neighborhood like it was his. He looked over his shoulder at the man in the cell. The man stared back.

"You aren't drinking," Jake said.

The man made a point of taking a long drink from the mug. "Happy?"

"Where do you live? Why don't you have ID? Where are you heading?"

The man smiled. "You have a lot of questions, Jake. Why aren't you in school?"

"It's bring your child to work day," Jake answered.

"And yet your father left you here alone while he's out working. That doesn't seem fair."

"It isn't fair," Jake agreed.

"Will he be back soon, do you think?"

"Who?"

"Your father."

"I don't know. Why?"

"Well, I have an illness and need medicine, but the other officer took my coat with my pills in the pocket. I need the pills."

"I don't know when he'll be back."

"Can you bring me my coat, then?"

"I don't think so."

"Can you just bring me my pills, then? You can push the bottle to me with the broom like before with the water."

"Okay. Did you see where they put your coat?"

"That locker, over there," the man replied motioning toward a set of lockers against a wall.

Jake went to the lockers and opened the one the man had pointed to. He removed the coat.

"Is this it," he asked?

"Yes," the man said, wincing like he was in pain. "Please bring the bottle over quickly. I am not well."

Jake rummaged through the pockets of the coat, feeling for a pill bottle, but finding nothing.

"There's no pills," he told the man.

The man was bending over at the waist now. He grimaced and was panting.

"There has to be. Check again, please. I hurt. I am going to faint."

Jake checked the pockets again, but still found nothing.

"Nothing. Maybe they took them out." He went back to the lockers and checked each for the pill bottle, but found nothing.

"Jake!"

Jake turned just in time to see the man collapse on the ground. In a panic, Jake rushed to the cell. He still did not get within arm's length of the bars, but he took a long look at the man. He could be faking, Jake thought, but then the man began to thrash on the ground. The man's head hit the bars, as he shook and spasmed. His head began to bleed. He isn't faking, Jake thought. He tried to calm himself. What should he do?

He went to his dad's desk and keyed the radio. "Dad! Dad, this is Jake. The guy in the cell is having a seizure. He says he needs pills. Over"

He waited for a response. He looked in the cell and the man continued to shake on the ground. His head hit the bars again and again. Jake thought the man might really be hurting himself. He needed to move the guy away from the bars. He tried the radio again.

"Dad, I don't know what to do. Come back to the station. I need help. Over!"

Again, silence.

Jake didn't know how to stop the seizure, but the least he could do was move the man away from the bars, so that he would stop hitting his head. He ran to the nail in the wall that held the keys to the cells, and then ran back to the cell. He fumbled with the keys for a moment until finding the right one to open the door. He turned the key and slid the door open. He grabbed the man's feet and pulled him away from the bars.

Away from the cell, on a desk, the fax machine whirred to life.

The radio squawked from Jake's dad's desk. From inside the cell Jake heard his dad's voice.

"Jake I'm almost back at the station. Don't do anything. I'll be there in a second."

Jake moved away from the man who had suddenly stopped shaking.

He made a move for the cell door, but the man was up and had his hand on Jake's wrist in an instant.

"Let go," Jake said.

"No, Jake."

Jake wrenched his wrist free and ran from the cell, the man right behind him. He grabbed Jake again. They struggled. Jake saw his dad pounding at the front door of the station. Jake twisted free again, but the man was between him and the door buzzer. There was nowhere he could run. The man slowly walked toward Jake.

A piece of paper slid free from the fax machine. On it was the image of a man. The man looked like a regular guy, but maybe a little too thin. Beneath the photo of the man were three words: **Wanted for Murder.**

The Treehouse

By Shawn Kobb

"Your mother is going to kill you if she sees what you've done."

My hand froze in place, the spoonful of Frosted Flakes halfway to my mouth. I had no idea what my dad was talking about and my mind raced through the possibilities.

What did he find? Was it something in my room? Did he look at the back of my underwear drawer? Was it that website I went to? I had no idea what it was going to be. They can't blame me for that. What did he know?

I decided to play it cool. I finished my bite of cereal before answering and tried to sound calm. "What are you talking about?"

My dad lowered the newspaper and peered at me from over the top. For a moment his face was serious and then he gave a little smile.

"Don't worry," he said, "I'm not going to tell her, but if she finds it, I'm not taking responsibility. Lucky for you she doesn't like to explore those woods like we do."

Was I sweating? Could my dad see it? What was he talking about?

"I really don't know what--"

"The treehouse, Jake." He flipped the newspaper back up so I couldn't see his face. "If you fall out of that thing and break your arm, I'm going to deny any knowledge of its existence."

"Treehouse?" I knew I was a terrible liar, but he had to hear the confusion in my voice. I didn't have any idea what he was talking about. "What treehouse?"

Dad lowered the paper again and squinted at me, but must have decided I wasn't willing to confess. "Look, I had a treehouse when I was a kid. I get it, but you know how your mother is. She'll freak out. Not to mention you aren't exactly the most coordinated kid."

"But dad--"

"I'm sorry, but you know it's true." He returned to looking at his paper. "And I don't even want to know where you and your friends found the wood to build it."

I could tell this conversation wasn't going anywhere. I truly had no idea what in the world my dad was talking about and he was *just* as convinced I was hiding something. I decided to drop it.

I shoveled the rest of my Frosted Flakes into my mouth as quickly as possible. Tony the Tiger would have been proud. I wanted to get outside before mom made it to breakfast. I took the bowl over to the sink and rinsed it out and put it into the dishwasher.

"Okay," I said. "I'll be careful."

"*Mm hmm.*" Dad didn't even look up, and he didn't sound convinced.

"I'm gonna meet Donny and Sam outside. We're riding bikes."

"Be careful."

I grabbed my hat from the hook next to the door as I ran out the backdoor. I thought I heard my mom calling my name as the door shut, but I kept moving. I had to figure out what my dad was talking about. A treehouse? It sounded awesome, but if I had one, it was news to me.

It was our first summer living in the new house. We'd moved here last fall right before school started up. It was rough at first to be in a new school in a new state. Heck, it was still pretty tough, but at least I'd made a few friends and I had to admit the new house was awesome.

We were right on the edge of town, but it felt like the wilderness. Dad said we had a bit over eight acres of land. I didn't really know how much an acre is, but it was clearly a lot. The area around the house was all nicely mowed with flowers and little brick paths and benches my mom loved.

But for me, the best part was once you went out the little gate in the backyard. Then you got to the wild part. My parents called it the woods, but if you ask me, it was practically a forest. There were trails, but not like the sort when you go to a park. These were made by deer (and my friends and I thought maybe even bears, though my dad said there weren't any bears in the entire state.)

There was so much to explore and Donny and Sam and I spent the first autumn exploring until it got too cold and snowy. Then we switched to building forts and having snowball fights. When spring came the woods turned colorful with little purple and yellow wildflowers and mosquitoes as big as my thumb buzzed around and left us with itchy bumps.

Now it was summer. School was out and all we wanted to do was explore. My mom worried about us back there, but my dad told her she should just be happy we wanted to be outside and not sitting in front of a computer screen playing games. Of course, we sometimes played on our cellphones out in the woods, but he didn't have to know that.

Mom almost never went back into the woods. When she did, it was when the whole family went out on little walks. Dad went back there occasionally, but he was usually too busy with work to have time. That left the woods all to me. I felt like a king back there.

It was still early in the day, but I could already tell it was going to be hot. Once I got out of the sun in the backyard and into the shade of the woods, it got much cooler and darker. Bits of sunlight broke through the tall branches of the maple and elm trees to dot the forest floor.

My friends and I had come to know our way around pretty well back there, but honestly even we got turned around sometimes. Some parts of the woods were really overgrown and it was easy to lose track of which way the house was. I searched everywhere trying to find the treehouse my dad mentioned.

He said it was back here and he must have thought my friends and I built it, but I honestly had zero idea what he was talking about. Was it really possible there was an old treehouse back here and we hadn't found it? It seemed impossible. I knew we'd explored every inch of these woods.

After a half hour or so, I found myself heading into the furthest, most hard to reach corner of the woods. We almost never went back here. There weren't any trails going into this part, the mosquitoes were extra bad, and there was poison ivy and sharp thorn bushes.

I carefully picked my way through the trees, being extra careful to watch out for the three pointy-leaf vines I knew were poison ivy. I can't imagine why dad would have come back here, but it was the only part left I hadn't completely explored. I knew I could only go a little bit further before my narrow trail ended in a wall of sharp, thorny bushes.

At least, that is how it used to be, but not today. There was a path through the bushes. And it wasn't the sort of tiny little path we usually found made by deer (and bears). It was wide enough I could walk with my arms outstretched at my sides without touching anything.

This wasn't here before. There was no way Donny, Sam, and I could have missed it. Where did it come from? Who had made it? It definitely wasn't Dad. Was someone else exploring my forest?

I was nervous. What if it was a homeless guy living back here? Maybe it was an escaped prisoner? I didn't think there were any prisons around, but I didn't know. Do bears make paths like this? Dad said we didn't have any, but he didn't really know.

I forced myself to take a deep breath and then moved forward. I wasn't a little kid. It was dumb to be scared of a trail in the woods. This was *my* forest. I was the king here.

The path went just a short way past the thorny bushes and then opened into a little clearing. The path was the only way in and the shrubs made a natural wall around a giant elm tree in the middle. The tree was so big that even if my friends and I held hands, I don't think we could have wrapped our arms around it.

Someone had nailed a series of uneven boards into the trunk and this simple ladder led up to the treehouse my Dad was so certain we had built. It wasn't huge, but it wasn't small either. The perfect size for about three people, if I had to guess. It stuck out from the tree so the ladder in the trunk led up into a hole in the floor. There was one big window in the wall facing me and it was covered from the inside by a piece of blue cloth hung like a curtain. It wasn't just any blue. It was a nice bright blue. My favorite color.

Above that big window someone had made a sign using black paint.

It read, Jake's Castle (No Adults Allowed).

When I read that I felt cold all over, like someone had poured a bucket of icy water over my head. No wonder Dad assumed I had built this.

Where had it come from? Had Donny and Sam built it as some sort of present or maybe as a joke? Had it always been here and they just missed it? Maybe the sign was just a coincidence? It wasn't like I was the only kid in the world named Jake.

Somehow I knew the answer to both questions was no. I didn't know where this treehouse had come from, but my friends didn't build it. I also knew it wasn't here before. The woods were big, but not that big.

As I stood staring up at the treehouse, I could see the blue curtain in the window moving ever so slightly in the breeze. In and out. In and out. It almost felt like the wooden treehouse was breathing. I found myself walking slowly toward the ladder. I didn't remember deciding to move closer, but suddenly I was standing at the base of the tree and looking up into the darkness of the entrance above.

Even as I placed my hands on the wooden rungs and started climbing, I heard a voice in my head asking if this was such a good idea. Was the treehouse safe to go in? What if the entire thing fell out of the tree when I got inside? What if there was a dangerous psycho in it, just waiting for me. Maybe it was a trap?

I heard these questions, but kept climbing. I pulled myself up into the treehouse. I stepped from the ladder and onto the floor. From the outside I thought it would be dark inside, but it wasn't. I couldn't tell where the light came from, but I could see just fine. It somehow felt much larger inside than I would have guessed from outside. Was it like an optical illusion? Outside it seemed just big enough for three people, but now that I was inside I was pretty sure I could have had six or seven or maybe even more friends in here. That is, if I had that many friends.

"Where did it come from?" I ran a hand along the wooden walls.

For a moment I thought I heard a voice answer. I couldn't tell where it came from. I spun around quickly but there was obviously nobody else in the treehouse. It wasn't like there was anywhere to hide.

"Who's there?" I called out, hoping I sounded braver than I felt. What if this was all a trick? What if some high school kids had built the treehouse and it was to trap little kids like me? My friends and I had heard high schoolers liked to pull pranks like throwing eggs at the elementary school kids.

Bring your friends.

It wasn't exactly like I heard the words. At least, not out loud. I just felt them somehow. It was like someone had spoken them directly inside my head.

I knew I had to have imagined it. There was no one else here.

But still, it felt so clear. Bring your friends. Someone...something had said it. I wasn't crazy, right?

I had to tell someone about this. I needed to show the treehouse to someone else so I could prove to myself I wasn't going nutso. I couldn't come back with Dad. (No Adults Allowed.) Some part of me knew that.

I had to find Donny and Sam. I would show them. They could help me figure out what to do.

I climbed carefully down the ladder. Right before my head was out of the treehouse, I heard the words in my head once again.

Bring your friends.

I climbed faster and dropped from the ladder a little higher than I should have. It hurt my feet, but I wanted to get out of there. I had to find Donny and Sam.

I pulled my bike to a skidding stop in front of Donny's house. I found my friend in the back yard mowing the lawn. Donny couldn't hear my yell over the loud roar of the lawnmower and I had to stand practically right in front of him to get his attention.

Donny turned off the mower. "Hey, Jake! What's up?"

"You've got to come with me. I've got to show you something."

Donny looked around the half-mowed yard. "I can't go anywhere until I finish this or my mom will kill me."

"It's an emergency, Donny," I could tell he was about to argue. "I'm serious."

Donny tilted his head to the side. "What is it?"

"It's...you just have to see. You won't believe me unless you see it. It's in my backyard."

"Is it a bear? Did you finally find one?"

I grabbed my friend by the arm and tried to pull him away from the mower. "It's not a bear. Come on, Donny. We've got to get Sam."

Donny pulled his arm away. "I told you. My mom will kill me."

I checked out how much yard was left to mow. "Just come with me and then I'll help you finish the yard work. We won't be gone long."

I knew Donny hated doing his chores. If there was any chance he could get me to help him do them, he'd risk making his mom mad. "You promise? She gets off work early today. If I'm not done by then, she'll ground me forever."

"I promise." I used my finger to cross my heart. "Now let's go."

We found Sam sitting on the couch watching TV. She was wearing her favorite Buffalo Bills baseball cap and had her ponytail pulled out through the back. Some of the other kids made fun of Sam for hanging out with us and dressing like a boy, but we didn't care. She was cool and she was tough. If we were honest, she was faster and stronger than either of us.

"Hey guys," She said as her mom let us into the living room. "What's up?"

"Jake's got something he has to show us," Donny said. I could tell he wasn't taking it very serious, but I didn't care as long as they came.

Sam looked to me. "What is it?"

Donny spoke before I had a chance. "It's no use. He won't say. He says we have to see it."

Ten minutes later we were dumping our bikes in my backyard and heading into the woods behind my house. Donny and Sam talked constantly, both trying to get me to say where we were going, but I knew I couldn't explain it.

Yeah, it was just a treehouse, but at the same time it wasn't. First of all, where'd it come from? Second, why did it have my name on it? Third, I'm pretty sure it talked to me. Donny and Sam were good friends, but they'd never believe me if I told them that.

As I led them toward the wild corner of the woods, Donny started to grumble. "I don't want to get poison ivy, Jake."

"You won't. Just watch where you step. Besides, we're almost there."

"Almost where, Jake?" Sam asked. "We've been back here. There's nothing here, but pricker bushes and mosquitoes. Besides..."

Her voice trailed off as we came to the neat path heading into the wild corner of woods. She knew it hadn't been there last time we'd come exploring this way.

"When did you do this?" she asked.

"How did you do it?" Donny asked. "It looks like something professional. Like in the park."

We stood looking at the path. From here, you couldn't see the treehouse. "That's just it. I didn't do it."

My friends looked at each other and then at me. "So who did? Your dad?"

I shook my head. "Just wait. It gets weirder."

I led them forward along the path and we came to the opening with the giant tree and the treehouse with my name printed over the window.

"Holy crap!" Donny said. "Awesome!"

"You built it?" Sam asked, moving forward to check it out.

"I told you. I didn't make it. That's just it. I don't know where it came from, but it wasn't here before."

"It had to have been," Donny said. "We just didn't see it. Besides, it has your name on it."

"How could we have missed it?" I asked, starting to feel angry my friends didn't believe me. I turned to Sam. "We explored all of the woods. How could we not have seen this?" I waved my hand toward the treehouse.

Sam actually seemed a little weirded out, but Donny had already started to climb the ladder.

"Wait, Donny," I said as I rushed forward. "Don't go in."

Donny dropped back to the ground and turned toward me. "Why not?"

"Yeah, Jake," Sam said quietly. "Why not?"

I had to say something, but I didn't want my only two friends to think I was crazy. "There's something...I don't know. Something wrong with it."

"What do you mean? It isn't safe?"

"Yeah," I said. "Well, no. I don't know."

"You're not making any sense," Sam said. "Why isn't it safe?"

Donny turned and started up the ladder again. "I'm not scared. I think Jake just wants it all to himself."

"No," I almost screamed it. "I think it's haunted."

Donny dropped to the ground again and turned to face me. He and Sam both stared at me for a second and then Donny burst into laughter. "Very funny. Oooh...a haunted treehouse. I'm so scared."

He turned and started to climb. Sam wasn't laughing. She was staring at me.

"Maybe we shouldn't, Donny," Sam said at last. "If we don't know where it came from--"

"Whatever," Donny said, as he continued to climb. "I'm checking it out. You babies can stay down there."

Donny's feet disappeared through the trapdoor in the floor of the treehouse. We could hear his voice coming from inside the treehouse.

"This is cool up here, guys. You have to check it out. It seems bigger in here than it did outside."

I felt silly. Had I just imagined everything? Sam looked at me and frowned.

"Is this some kind of joke?" She asked.

"No," I mumbled, but felt bad Sam thought I'd tried to scare them. "I just--"

"What'd you guys say?" It was Donny's voice, coming from inside the treehouse.

"We didn't say anything," Sam yelled up at him. "What did you hear?"

"Who said that? Who's in here?" Donny's voice began to rise in pitch and he sounded like he was panicking. "Who is that?"

"Donny?" I shouted and ran to the ladder and looked up, but I couldn't see anything inside of the treehouse. "Get out of there, Donny!"

Suddenly there was a scream from inside the treehouse. It was Donny, but I'd never heard him make a sound like that before. The scream ended just as suddenly as it began and then it was very quiet.

"Donny!" I shouted up, but nobody answered. I looked back to Sam and her eyes were about to pop out of her head she was so scared. "I'm going up."

"No, Jake!" Sam shouted. "We need to get help."

"You get help. I'm going up."

Sam looked at me for a second and then took off running down the trail back into the woods. I knew she'd go get my parents. If Donny was hurt, my dad would know what to do.

I took a deep breath and forced myself to start climbing the ladder. There was no sound coming from inside the treehouse. *Almost* no sound. I thought I could hear the wind coming and going in through the window. In and out. Almost like breathing.

I pulled my head up through the hole in the floor and into the treehouse. Why was it so dark? It hadn't been dark before.

* * *

Sam ran as fast as she ever had. She jumped over branches and swerved around trees. She had to get to Jake's house. She'd get his parents and bring them to the treehouse. Whatever happened to Donny, they'd be able to help. She just had to get them before something happened to Jake as well. She'd explain and...

Explain what, exactly? She slowed her run to a jog and then to a walk. What would she tell Jake's parents? They found a treehouse and it ate their friend? It sounded like a terrible prank.

A prank.

Sam stopped walking. Could it be?

Were Donny and Jake pulling a stupid prank on her? Normally they treated her just like a regular friend. They didn't act differently around her because she was a girl. But every once in a while one of them would say something or do something to remind her she wasn't really one of the boys. Would they pull a mean joke like this on her? She didn't want to believe it, but what was more likely? A haunted treehouse ate her friends or that they were trying to trick her?

Sam felt tears start to come to her eyes, but she wiped them away. Part of her just wanted to go home and wait for Jake and Donny to show up and apologize for being jerks. But a bigger part of her wanted to show them she wasn't afraid and she wasn't dumb.

Sam turned around and walked back through the woods to the treehouse. She thought about how she would find them sitting in the treehouse laughing at her and how scared she had been. If they did laugh at her, she'd punch them right in the face. Then she would see how funny they thought it was to try and scare her.

She reached the little path through the wild part of the woods. A small part of her brain asked how the two boys had managed to make such nice trail, but she ignored it.

Sam started yelling before she even entered the little clearing where the giant elm tree stood with its treehouse.

"Very funny, guys! You know, I should have gotten your dad and brought him here, then we'd see how funny..." Sam's voice trailed off. Something was wrong. Something was different.

She studied the treehouse. Was it that big before? She thought it had been smaller for some reason. And the curtain in the window. Sam could have sworn it was blue, but it was definitely red now. Not just any red, but a bright fire engine red...her favorite color. How could she not have noticed that before?

And the sign above the window. That was definitely different. She knew that for sure. It was hand painted, just like before, but now it read:

Samantha's Treehouse (No Adults Allowed)

Did her friends change it? They couldn't have. For one, the paint was completely dry. Second, it wasn't like they could fit her full name in the same space that said *Jake* before. How did they do it? Why?

"Jake? Donny?" Sam called up to the treehouse. If they were up there, they were dead silent. She couldn't even hear them whispering. It was almost impossible for Donny to stay quiet for long. She expected to hear him start laughing at any second, but it didn't come. Had they left?

Sam stood at the base of the tree and rested her hands on the ladder leading inside the treehouse. Were they up there?

She felt scared, but knew it was stupid. They'd probably left. Sam didn't know why they possibly thought this was a funny prank. Maybe they weren't as good of friends as she thought. But she had to go up and make sure they weren't inside.

Sam grabbed the highest board she could and pulled herself into the treehouse one step at a time. She could hear the wind outside moving in and out of the treehouse. In and out.

It almost sounded like breathing.

A Belief in Monsters

By David Kobb

Malcom thinks there is something in his basement. He won't go down there alone. He doesn't like going down there even if his mom or dad is down there. He would be happy if he never had to go into the basement again.

The basement walls are bare cinderblocks covered in a single layer of green paint. There are cobwebs everywhere. Worst of all, the basement is lit by a single dingy lightbulb hanging in the middle of the room. The bulb's weak light doesn't quite reach into the corners of the room and the dark shapes come alive in Malcom's mind.

Malcom thinks there is something in the basement. He thought he saw it once. He was alone and playing. This was before he was afraid of the basement. He was bouncing a ball, and didn't notice the basement door was open. The ball got away from him and rolled down the stairs. He hit the light switch at the top of the basement steps, turning on the single light. The bulb buzzed like a fly trapped in a glass jar. He climbed down the stairs, the thin wooden steps creaking under him, and went to get his ball. That was when he first thought he saw it.

It was just a quick glance out of the corner of his eye. Something large and dark, looming in the shadows and glaring at him. It had spiny hair that looked sharp to the touch. Its eyes glowed green. As quick as he saw it, it was gone.

His parents didn't believe him, of course. Parents never believe their children about monsters. They told him that there was no such thing as monsters. They said it was all his imagination, but Malcom knows something a lot of kids don't. Parents aren't always right.

Something is wrong with the dishwashing machine in the kitchen. Malcom's dad is working on it. He asks Malcom to get a screwdriver from the red toolbox in the basement.

Malcom tells his dad that he doesn't want to get the screwdriver from the basement. His dad asks him why not. Malcom explains that he thinks there is a monster in the basement. His dad tells him that he is old enough not to believe in monsters and then tells him that he must get the screwdriver.

Malcom walks to the basement door and swings it open. The door opens with a *creaaaak*. He reaches his hand into the dark at the top of the stairs, feeling around for the light switch. He's sure that at any second a large, hairy, clawed hand will wrap its fingers around his small hand and tug him into the basement dark. Instead, his fingers brush the light switch and Malcom flips the light on.

The basement light flickers to life for a brief moment and then flashes out. Malcom heads back to the kitchen and tells his dad about the light burning out. His dad tells him to find a flashlight in the living room and then go get the screwdriver.

Malcom walks into the living room and tells his mom that his dad wanted him to get a screwdriver from the basement, but that he doesn't want to. She asked why, and he explains to her that he thinks there is something terrible lurking in the basement. His mother laughs and tells him that he is too old to believe in such nonsense. She helps him find the flashlight and then asks him to hurry and help his dad.

Malcom stands just outside the basement steps and turns the flashlight on. He takes one hesitant step and then another. He holds his breath, certain that he'll meet his doom at any moment. The pale white light from the flashlight does little to brighten the terrible dark of the basement. He reaches the bottom stair and takes a few cautious steps into the basement. The flashlight flares bright and then suddenly goes dark.

Malcom hears a gurgling breath that sounds like water going down a half-blocked drain. He feels it hot against the back of his neck. It smells like warm garbage. He hears the sound of razor sharp claws being dragged across cinderblock walls. He feels bristling fur brush against his cheek.

Malcom thinks there is something in the basement.

Malcom thinks his parents don't know everything.

Malcom thinks there is something terrible right behind him.

Malcom is right.

Back Scratches

By David Kobb

"That's it, right there," Ganesh Gupta said as he leaned back against his mother's sharp fingernails.

"Will you ever tire of having your back scratched?" his mother asked with exasperation.

"I doubt it. It feels so nice," he said.

"I'm always so worried that I'm going to scratch you raw," she said with a frown.

Ganesh closed his eyes. "I wish you would. The harder you scratch the better it feels."

"You're a strange one," she said with a smile, "but you're my son and I like to make you happy."

Ganesh had enjoyed having his back scratched for as long as he could remember. One of his earliest memories was sitting on his mother's lap as a small child and watching television as she gently scratched his back. He wasn't sure why he liked to have his back scratched so much, only that he did. Maybe it was because it was always such a peaceful time. His mom worked a lot and was almost never home. Ganesh spent most of his time with his nanny, Leona. The few moments he got with his mom each day, she usually spent running around on her cell phone. The only time he could get her to sit down and pay attention to him was while she scratched his back.

"Mom," Ganesh said, "I don't want to go to sleep tonight."

Ganesh had been having the same nightmares for a few weeks. There was a hideous monster in his closet, and it waited for him to go to sleep and would then slowly creep toward him. He could see the scene from above, like he was floating in the air above the bed. He saw himself asleep, and the shadowy monster gently push open the closet door. It was like the creature was made of night. It melted into the shadows on the bedroom walls and would slink slowly along until it was next to his bed. It had glowing purple eyes and needles in place of fingers. He always woke up before it got to him, but he was afraid that one night he wouldn't wake up in time.

"Of course you have to sleep. Don't be a silly boy."

"But the nightmares, mom. He's going to get me tonight. I know it!"

"There's nothing to get you. You know that. Whenever you get scared just think of a happy memory."

"But it's Friday. I don't have school tomorrow," he pleaded.

"Doesn't matter. You're not staying up all night. A smart boy like you needs his rest. The world is scary enough. You don't need to put monsters in closets to make it even worse."

"But, mom..."

"No!" she said and gave his back one last scratch.

"Ow!" Ganesh said, as he jerked away from his mother.

"Oh, sweetie, did I scratch you too hard? I'm sorry."

"It's okay," he said, rubbing the pain away from his back.

"No more talk of nightmares and monsters, okay?"

"Okay, mom. Do you think you could come in and scratch my back if I have the nightmare? If you're still up, at least?"

"Okay, but only this one more time."

Ganesh went to school, but couldn't concentrate in his classes. He kept thinking about his nightmares. The last time he had the dream was a couple of days earlier in the week. In that one, the creature had gotten so close to him that he was certain it would get him. Then, at the very last second, he woke up. He must have screamed in his sleep because when he woke up his mother was standing over his bed with a concerned look on her face. She scratched his back until he fell back to sleep.

Ganesh had brushed his teeth, and was reading in bed when his mom came to his bedroom door.

"Lights out," she said.

"Can I read a few more pages?"

"No. It's time for bed. Besides, it's probably those scary stories you read that give you the nightmares."

Ganesh put his book on his bedside table.

"No nightmares tonight. I won't allow it," she said with a smile.

"No nightmares," Ganesh said trying to will it into being true.

Ganesh's mom kissed him on the forehead and then turned the light off. She left the room, closing the door behind her.

Ganesh closed his eyes, but didn't want to sleep. He knew tonight was the night. Tonight the creature would get him.

Ganesh was asleep in his bed. His bedroom was dark and quiet and he was snoring softly. There was a slow and subtle movement in the bedroom. The closet door gently opened. A dark creature crept out of the closet. It climbed up the wall and slid along the ceiling almost like it was a part of it. It moved along the ceiling until it was over Ganesh's bed. Its purple eyes glowed brightly in the dark. It lowered itself from the ceiling. It lifted an arm, its needle-like fingers drifting close to Ganesh. The needle points glimmered in the sparse moonlight that leaked in through the window curtains. The claws moved closer to Ganesh. Closer. Closer and...

Ganesh awoke with a gasp. It happened. It touched him. His breath came in short and shallow bursts. He tried to calm himself. He heard a door open in the dark room and then soft footsteps cross his bedroom floor.

"Oh, mom," he said, still panting. "It was terrible. It touched me. I'm so glad I'm awake."

The footsteps ended at the side of the bed and Ganesh felt gentle scratches at his back.

"Thanks, mom. That feels nice." He started to calm down. "A little harder" he asked?

The scratches got harder.

Then the scratches got even harder.

"Oh, that's a little too hard, mom."

The scratches got even harder!

"Ow, mom. That hurts! That's too hard!"

The scratches got even harder. The nails dug into Ganesh's back like needles. Ganesh heard his pajama shirt rip as the nails, like needles, shredded through it. He felt his skin tear from the clawing at his back. He screamed in pain!

Suddenly his bedroom door opened and his light turned on. In the doorway stood his mother.

"What is it?" she asked. "The nightmare again?"

"Mom!" Ganesh sobbed. "Why did you do that?"

"Do what?" his mother asked, a confused look on her face.

"Why did you hurt me? Why did you scratch me so hard?"

"When? Just now?" she asked.

"Please don't hurt me again. My back hurts so bad."

"Sweetie, I haven't touched you. You had a nightmare again."

Ganesh's mother moved to the side of his bed. "It was just a dream," she said. "You're alright. You're safe."

"Do I look okay!?" he yelled, moving the blanket away from his back.

His pajama shirt had been ripped to tatters. The skin on his back was cut open and blood oozed out.

"Oh, no!" His mother said, putting her hand to her mouth. "What happened? Sweetie I didn't do that. That wasn't me."

Only then did Ganesh remember his nightmare. The creature had finally touched him.

New House

By David Kobb

Isabell Adams' new house reminded her of a rotting gravestone, half crumbled into cemetery dirt. Fuzzy green moss smothered the roof, and creeping vines clutched at the windows like grasping hands. She had no idea why, but her mother loved the place.

"Isn't it great?" Mrs. Adams said, beaming with pride. "And it's all ours. It was dirt cheap, too."

Isabell sneered at the house, and then turned the sneer on her mother. "Yeah, mom. It's *great*."

"Oh, sarcasm. How *original*. You're such a tween," Mrs. Adams said, matching her daughter's sarcastic tone.

"It was cheap, because it's a death trap, mom," Isabell pouted.

Mrs. Adams took a breath. "Listen, I know you didn't want to move, but we did, and there's no going back. You might try to make the best of it." Mrs. Adams smiled hopefully.

"But it's falling apart, mom! I think I got tetanus just by *looking* at it."

"It's all we could afford, okay? We'll fix it up in no time. I bet the inside is nice!"

The inside of the house wasn't any better. As the sun moved to hide behind the tall willow trees that surrounded the house, Isabell and her mother spent most the night unpacking their moving boxes.

"Okay," Mrs. Adams said, wiping sweat from her brow, "let's take a break for dinner. Pizza?"

Isabell did not feel like eating. All she wanted to do was take a shower and sleep in her old bed at her old house. "Pizza's fine," she grumbled.

Mrs. Adams pulled out her cell phone and found a nearby pizza place. She called and ordered a large pepperoni and mushroom, which was Isabell's favorite.

"They said it'd be half an hour," Mrs. Adams said, hanging up the phone. "Until then, we clean and unpack."

Mrs. Adams was downstairs, still trying and failing to make the living room livable. Isabell explored the house's upper level. She found a small door, just a couple of feet tall, in the hallway near the stairs. She opened it and saw a dark crawlspace. The little light that leaked in from the hallway was just enough for Isabell to see that the crawlspace was filled with spider webs. Wind from the outside whistled in from a crack in the wall and played a funeral lament. Her skin crawled and she quickly closed the door. That crawlspace was like a nightmare she often had – a dark space, tight like a coffin, and crawling with spiders.

After shutting the crawlspace door, she began to walk away. After just a couple of steps, she heard a click. She turned around and saw that the crawlspace door was open. She walked back over, grabbed the small latch on the door, and pulled it shut again. She frowned at it for a moment and then turned and walked away. Again, after a few steps, she heard a click. She stopped, turned her head, and watched as the crawlspace door crept open. She ran downstairs.

"Mom!" she yelled.

"What is it?" her mom asked, head half buried in a moving box.

"I hate this place! There's a creepy door that won't stay shut upstairs, and the entire place is covered in spider webs. My friends aren't here!" Isabell cried.

"I'm sorry we had to move, honey, but this is where I found a job. Since your dad passed away, money has been tight. This place is all we could afford. We'll fix it up and you'll make friends at your new school. You'll see. Everything will be okay. What's that about a door?"

Before Isabell could answer, there was a pounding on the front door. Both Isabell and her mother jumped. Then they laughed.

"Pizza guy," Mrs. Adams guessed, smiling.

Isabell and her mother went to the front door, peeked out the window next to it and saw the pizza delivery guy standing on the porch.

"Hi," Mrs. Adams said, as she opened the front door. "Oops, forgot to grab the money." She turned and jogged away.

The deliver guy looked at Isabell, "You guys just move in?" he asked.

"Yeah. Today," she said.

"It's been a long time since anyone's lived here," he said, scanning the outside of the house with a hint of fear in his eyes.

"I don't like it. The house is creepy," she said.

"Well of course it's creepy. After everything that happened here..." he trailed off.

Isabell looked at him, curious, "What do you mean?"

"You're not from here, are you?" he asked.

"No."

"So you wouldn't know about it?"

"About what?" she asked, her body tense.

Before he could say anything, Mrs. Adams was back.

"Here you go," she said handing over the money.

"Any change?" he asked.

"Nope, it's all yours."

"Thanks," he said.

As Mrs. Adams began to close the door, the delivery guy stuck his foot between the door and frame. Mrs. Adams' eyes widened slightly as she let out a small gasp.

"What?" Mrs. Adams asked.

"You two be careful in this house, okay?" He looked at them, dead serious, and then slid his foot out from between the door.

"Thanks, we will be," Mrs. Adams said as she closed the door, locking it behind her.

"What did he mean, mom?" Isabell asked.

"What a weirdo," Mrs. Adams said.

"Mom, what did he mean be careful?" Isabell asked again.

"Oh, it's probably nothing. He was just a weirdo. Or maybe he just meant we should be careful because it's an old house and needs some work. You know, rusty nails and stuff."

Isabell looked at her mother doubtfully. "I don't think so. While you were getting the money, he was telling me about something that happened here. He said no one's lived here for a long time."

"He was just messing with us. We're done talking about it."

"But, mom..." Isabell began to protest.

"I said we're done," Mrs. Adams said with a frown. "Let's eat."

Outside, in the distance, a storm began to rumble. It slowly grew closer as the daylight died and cold night assumed its place.

Isabell tossed and turned on an air mattress in her new bedroom. The moving van with her real bed hadn't arrived yet. She tried closing her eyes, but each time she did a new noise would open them. Pipes rattled in the basement, and some animal scurried about in the attic. Something unseen moved in the walls. Isabell opened her eyes and watched dancing shadows on the ceiling. The moonlight streaming through the willow trees caused the shadows to take monstrous shapes as they jumped and bled across the walls. Every creak in the floorboard was a killer in the hallway. Every tree branch that brushed against her bedroom window was someone eagerly tapping at the pane, signaling their desire to come in. Every shadowed corner of her room hid a demon with sour breath and glistening teeth.

Worst of all, she had to pee.

She gathered her courage and when she couldn't hold it any longer, she moved to her bedroom door and pressed her ear against the cold wood and listened. Nothing. She turned the handle and pushed the door open. The hallway outside her room was dark. She felt the wall for a light switch but there wasn't one. She tiptoed past her mom's bedroom, and heard soft snoring from inside. She kept going and made it to the bathroom door before remembering that it wasn't working yet. She had to use the bathroom downstairs.

She turned around and headed toward the staircase at the other end of the hallway. She stayed as far from the crawlspace door as possible. She eyed the door suspiciously as she passed. It was closed.

She crept down the stairs, each one creaking as she put her weight on it. She walked toward to the bathroom, through the living room, to the kitchen and stopped.

Her mother was in the kitchen.

Isabell froze. Her mother stood beside the kitchen window, staring out. The moonlight through the swaying willow tree branches painted moving shadows across her mother's face. A draft from somewhere in the leaky old house cut through Isabell's pajamas and she shivered.

"Mom?" Isabell ventured.

Her mother stood still, straight and rigid.

Was she sleepwalking, Isabell asked herself? Her mother had done it before, at their old house, and afterward Isabell did some Googling. She read that some people thought it was safer not to wake a sleepwalker.

The wind from the storm outside picked up, and the same sad musical whistling she had heard from the crawlspace earlier now played throughout the house. In the distance, thunder rumbled. Lightning crashed outside the window near where her mother stood. Isabell gasped! In that quick flash of lightning Isabell saw her mother's face. Her lips were twisted in a terrible grin, teeth wet and sharp.

Isabell no longer had to pee. At that moment, she wanted nothing more than to be under the covers in her old bedroom at her old house. As quietly as she could, she slunk back to the staircase and began to climb. It was only then that she realized, if her mother was downstairs, then who was snoring in her bedroom?

Reaching the upstairs hallway, Isabell walked quickly to her bedroom. As she passed the crawlspace, she noticed that the door yawned open wide like a screaming mouth. Isabell rushed to her room, throwing the door shut behind her. She slumped against it, her breath coming in quick bursts.

What was going on, Isabell wondered in a near panic? Did she just imagine snores from her mother's bedroom? Why was her mother grinning like that? She thought about the pizza delivery guy's warning and how her mother blew it off. What was going on with that crawlspace?

Isabell wished that her new bedroom door had a lock like her old one had. But then, she wondered, who would she have been locking out? Her mom? Her mom wouldn't hurt her. She had just freaked herself out. It was the new house and the storm, she decided. She was scared over nothing. With the noise of the storm, she couldn't be sure what she heard. She probably imagined the snoring from her mom's room. Obviously no one was sleeping in the room, since her mom was downstairs sleep walking. The crawlspace door probably just had a bad latch, and the wind blew it open, she decided. In the light of day it would all add up to one big scary nothing.

She opened her eyes. The sun jumped through the bedroom window and played on the walls, replacing the shadows of the night before. In the daylight, the events of the previous night almost seemed funny. A sunny and cloudless morning replaced the previous night's storm. In a tree near the house, a robin sang. Isabell sat up in her bed and stretched.

"Isabell, time to get up!" her mother's voice sounded from downstairs.

Isabell crawled out of bed, running her fingers through her hair. The sun coming through the window was warm on her skin. She wondered, what had she ever been afraid of? She decided to take a different look at the house, and at the move. It was a new day, and with a new day came new possibilities. She had made a bunch of nothing into something and scared herself. She was in a new town and a new house, and she would be going to a new school soon. She decided to look at it all like it was a new adventure.

She opened her bedroom door and started down the hallway.

"Isabell hurry up, breakfast is ready!" her mom called, starting to sound annoyed.

Isabell was nearly at the stairs when suddenly the crawlspace door flew open. A hand shot out and clutched her leg!

Isabell shrieked, and tried to kick off the fingers around her ankle. Something was in the crawlspace. It had her!

She gave one sudden jerk of her leg and freed it from the monster's grasp and turned to run.

"Isabell!" The voice whispered urgently from behind. "It's me."

She knew the voice. Isabell felt a chill run down her spine as she slowly turned to look behind her.

There, in the crawlspace crouched her mother, bits of spider webs clung to her hair.

"Shhhh!" her mother said with her finger to her lips. She reached out a hand and beckoned Isabell toward the crawlspace. "Come. Before she comes looking for you. I heard her voice, too."

Cool

By Shawn Kobb

Cassie slowly pulled the books she needed from her locker. If anyone had been paying attention to her it would have been comical how slowly she grabbed first her math book and then deliberately put it back and replaced it with the English textbook she needed.

Fortunately for Cassie, nobody ever paid attention to her.

She was stalling, her eyes peeking through little holes punched in the steel door of her locker. They were coming. If she timed it just right, it would seem so natural...

They were almost to her, talking loudly to each other and then laughing hysterically as though they were anywhere other than Greenbrook Junior High School on a Tuesday morning.

Cassie waited until the group of girls was just on the other side of her locker before suddenly slamming the door shut, leaving her face to face with Tabitha--by far the coolest girl in school.

"Oh hey," Cassie said, not recognizing the casual, friendly voice coming from her mouth. "I was just headed to English. Are you on your way?"

Cassie knew full well Tabitha was going to the same class. They sat next to each other every day, not that the super popular girl ever acknowledged her. Instead, Tabitha spent her time whispering loudly to her friends and texting on her phone. It drove Mr. Tomkins absolutely crazy, but every time he called on her, she had the perfect answer. Every time he confiscated her phone, she showed up the next day with a new one.

Tabitha stood in front of Cassie, her perfectly shaped lips forming a crooked little smile. Tabitha's three friends stared at Cassie like she was some sort of bug. One they were eager to squash.

"It's Cassie, right?" Tabitha asked.

Cassie's heart started to pound so hard in her chest, she was sure the other girls would hear it. "Yeah." Her voice was barely above a whisper. Why had she decided today, when the school year was almost finished, to finally try to talk to the Cool Girls?

"As a matter of fact, I've decided to give Mr. Tomkins a little break today."

"A break?"

"That's right," Tabitha looked to her friends. "Isn't it girls?"

The others smiled in response. All wore the same blood red lipstick. Cassie's mom let her wear a tiny bit of blush, but that was it. Her parents would kill her if she tried to leave the house in lipstick.

"You're not going to English class?" Cassie asked.

"No, we're not." Tabitha paused and looked Cassie from head to toe and then gave another crooked little smile. "How would you like to come with us?"

It must have been her imagination, but Cassie could have sworn the other three Cool Girls repeated it. *Come with us.* But their lips never moved. They only smiled, their eyes locked on Cassie.

"Where are you going?" Cassie asked, holding her books tight to her chest.

"You won't be needing those." One of Tabitha's friends took Cassie's books from her. "It was this locker, right?"

Tabitha turned to Cassie's locked and reached for the padlock and pulled it off. She handed it to Cassie.

"It looks like you forgot to lock it. You should be more careful." Tabitha smiled, her teeth gleamed white from behind her red lips. They were perfect.

Cassie looked at the lock in her hand. Had she forgotten to close the lock? She must have.

The girl who took Cassie's books shoved them roughly into the locker and slammed the door. Just then, the bell rang. They were already late to class and for the first time Cassie noticed the hallway had cleared out around them while they had been talking.

"I don't know, Tabitha. I think we have a quiz and..."

Tabitha put her arm around Cassie's waist and started walking. The other girls followed along right behind. "Don't you worry. You know I have old Tomkins wrapped around my little finger."

"Yeah, I guess, but--"

"In fact," Tabitha said, interrupting, "there he is. We'll just let him know we won't be able to make it today."

The popular girl was right. Their teacher was coming around the corner and walking straight toward them. He was a heavyset man, with a bushy mustache that made up for the lack of hair on his head. He always seemed to be sweating and red-faced even sitting at his desk.

"Girls," he said as he saw them. "You are late. Get to your seats immediately and I won't mark you tardy." His eyes paused on Cassie, clearly confused as to what she was doing with Tabitha and her gang. Cassie was one of the best students in the class and never caused trouble.

"Not today, I'm afraid." Tabitha's voice was calm and unconcerned. "It's too nice of a day to sit in a classroom."

Mr. Tomkins stopped walking and turned red. Well, redder. "Excuse me, young lady? You get in that room right now or you can go to the principal's office instead."

Tabitha stopped suddenly, still clutching on to Cassie by the waist. The girl was surprisingly strong and Cassie didn't think she couldn't have escaped if she wanted to. The other Cool Girls stopped in sync.

For a second Tabitha didn't say anything, she only locked eyes with the teacher. Mr. Tomkins was much taller than them, but at that moment Tabitha somehow seemed to loom over him. Mr. Tomkins wasn't blinking and his normally red face began to turn pale. Cassie thought he might pass out.

"No, Mr. Tomkins. We will not be in class today. And that's okay, isn't it?"

Her voice was relaxing, soothing. It was like she was talking to a baby.

Tomkins nodded slowly. "That's okay."

"In fact, you won't even mark us as absent. We were there. And we all scored one hundred percent on the quiz. Isn't that right?"

"It is. Very well done girls." Their teacher spoke slowly.

Had Tabitha hypnotized Mr. Tomkins? *Is that even a real thing?* Cassie wondered. She thought hypnosis was just something in movies, but how else could she explain it?

"Come on, Cassie," Tabitha looped her arm through Cassie's and pulled her along and they left Mr. Tomkins standing in the hallway, a sleepy expression on his face and just a little bit of drool hanging from his bottom lip.

Cassie didn't understand what was going on, but she knew one thing. She did not want to hang out with Tabitha and the other Cool Girls. They were not exciting. They were not fun. They were...what? Strange? Weird? Dangerous?

The other girls chatted and giggled as they walked, but Cassie didn't hear anything they said. She wasn't listening. She had to get away from them. Could she pretend to be sick? Maybe she remembered she was going home early that day because her grandmother had died and there was a funeral and...

"Cassie!"

She realized they had stopped in front of a door Cassie didn't recognize. A sign read "Authorized Personnel Only" on it. Tabitha had led them to a corner of the school students rarely visited. They were near the area where the janitors had their offices and kept their supplies.

"What are we doing here?"

Tabitha laughed and turned to the others. "I told you she wasn't listening." The popular girl turned back to

Cassie and gave her a wicked smile. "This is our secret place. We come here to get away from all of this." She waved her hand dismissing the rest of the school.

"But I don't think we're supposed to go--"

"Don't be such a little wimp, Cassie," Tabitha's face turned so scary and so mean for just a second before the little smile reappeared and she was beautiful once again. "We can do whatever we want. We're the Cool Girls."

The other two girls laughed and one of them pulled the door open. It was dark on the other side and the hallway quickly stretched out of view.

"You want to be one of us, don't you Cassie?"

Cassie found it impossible to look away from Tabitha's eyes. She'd never seen anything quite like them. At first she thought there were green, but the longer she stared the darker they seemed to become. Blue, then brown, until they were almost black with no distinction between the pupil and iris.

Cassie nodded. "Yeah, I want to be one of you."

Tabitha smiled and pulled her into the tunnel. The other two girls followed behind and pulled the door shut. It was so dark Cassie was certain they'd trip over something and fall, but Tabitha plunged ahead as though it was as bright as day. She pulled Cassie along with her.

A humming sound in the hallway grew louder the further they walked. The other girls didn't seem to notice other than to talk and giggle even louder. After a minute of walking, they entered a large room. The humming had transformed into a loud buzz and it was coming from some large machines in the center of the room. Control panels were covered with little red and green lights. The colored lights at least made it possible for Cassie to see, although it made her skin look sort of purple.

"Where are we?" Cassie asked.

"You're in our little clubhouse," Tabitha said. "We only bring special guests here. Isn't that right girls?"

The other two giggled and stared at Cassie. One of them ran her tongue over her perfect red lips. The other stroked Cassie's hair.

"What do you do in your club?" Cassie asked quietly. She didn't really want to know. All she wanted to do was to go back to class. She wanted to forget all about being a Cool Girl. They weren't cool at all. They were weird. They were rude and they were mean.

"I told you," Tabitha said. "We bring special people here. And then we usually have them for a snack."

A snack? Cassie thought. They skipped class and came to this creepy room just because they were hungry? That's what this was all about?

"I didn't bring any food," Cassie said, before coming up with an idea to leave. "I have some stuff in my locker though. If you want, I could run and get it and bring it back." Cassie started to turn back the way they came, hoping they'd let her go. She would run straight to Mr. Tomkins, apologize for everything, and then never talk to Tabitha or her creepy friends again.

Tabitha's hand shot out and grabbed Cassie by the arm. She was so strong. Her hand was crushing and Cassie yelped in pain.

"That's not necessary, Cassie. You don't understand."

The three girls had circled around her now. Cassie couldn't see the others, but she heard a smacking sound, even over the buzz of the machinery. They were licking their lips.

"You've already brought us our snack."

Tabitha flashed her beautiful smile again, but Cassie noticed it was changing just like her eye color seemed to change. Tabitha's white teeth were perfect, but as she watched it seemed like the two incisors grew longer and longer. They were pointed like her German Shepherd's. They went past her bottom lip and didn't even fit into her mouth any more.

"You want to be one of us, Cassie? You want to be one of the Cool Girls?" Tabitha's voice was hardly recognizable. It was deeper and the words were slurred because of her giant teeth. "You can be. You can be one of us. Or you can be food. Which is it, Cassie?"

Cassie's breath came in sharp gasps. Her heart pounded in her chest. She whipped her head around to the other three girls and saw they had the same dark eyes and huge teeth as Tabitha. They were drooling and looked at her like she was a steak in a fancy restaurant.

Cassie looked at Tabitha. She looked into those deep, dark eyes and suddenly felt calm. She thought of how lonely she was at school. She didn't have friends. The teachers didn't know her name. Her parents didn't have time for her. She knew what she wanted.

"I want to be cool."

Tabitha smiled, her long teeth reflecting the red and green lights of the machines. She lunged forward, those incredible teeth coming straight at Cassie's throat.

A Selfie with Bigfoot

By David Kobb

Ethan spent the entire morning repacking his backpack. It was the first time that he would be camping without adult supervision, and he couldn't decide what to bring and what to leave at home.

"You're only going to be out for one night, buddy. You sure you need all of that?" Ethan's dad, asked, looking down at the pile of camping gear Ethan had spread across the floor.

Ethan studied the pile of gear surrounding him. "I don't know. Better to have something and not need it than to need something and not have it, right dad?" he asked. He then began repacking his bag for the third time.

Ethan's cellphone, a gift he received for his birthday this year, buzzed on his bed. Ethan's dad looked over at it. "You're not bringing your phone at least, right?"

"Of course I'm taking it, dad. I've got a GPS app. I've got an app that tells me how to start fires in different ways, like with rocks and sticks and stuff. And I need to take photos?"

"Okay, okay," Ethan's dad said, shaking his head. "Take your phone, but remember, you've got to carry all of that weight."

Ethan was beginning to wish that he hadn't packed so much. He only carried his pack to his dad's car and already his shoulders were sore. At least, he thought, they were just camping at grandpa's property and they wouldn't have too far to hike.

The only way Ethan's parents would allow him to camp with his friends without adult supervision was if they did so on his Grandpa's property. His Grandpa owned a large patch of land in northern Michigan. Ethan had been there before, but not since he was a little kid. He remembered it being very beautiful.

Ethan stashed his pack in the trunk of his dad's car and then got in the passenger seat. Ethan and his dad drove off and picked up Ethan's friends Michael and Bennett.

Ethan turned in the passenger seat up front and looked at his friends in the back. "What did you bring to eat?" he asked Bennett.

"Can of beef and vegetable soup, chocolate bars, marshmallows and graham crackers for s'mores and some trail mix. You?"

"Beef jerky, a pack of dehydrated spaghetti and sauce, some cereal. What about you Michael?"

Michael smacked his forehead. "I forgot to bring anything."

Ethan's dad looked at Michael in the rearview mirror, "You didn't bring any food?"

Michael hung his head. "Forgot."

Ethan shrugged his shoulders, "No big deal, you can share what we brought. Right Bennett?"

"We've got your back, bud," Bennett said, giving Michael a soft punch to the shoulder.

"You want me to turn around, so you can grab some food?" Ethan's dad asked Michael.

"No, I'll be fine sharing with the guys," Michael replied.

Moments later, Ethan's dad slowed the car and turned onto a long dirt drive. A little ways in they passed a large white farmhouse.

"That your Grandpa's house?" Bennett asked Ethan.

"Yep," Ethan replied.

Ethan's dad added, "He's not home though. He's out on a fishing trip. Said he probably won't be home until sometime tomorrow. You boys will be on your own out there."

"No problem, dad," Ethan said confidently.

Ethan's dad pulled the car over and parked. Everyone got out. A fresh wind blew across Ethan's face. The sun was high in the sky and shone brightly all around.

"It's a great day to go camping," Ethan said to no one in particular.

Ethan's dad popped the car trunk and all three boys fetched their packs.

Bennett slung his pack across his back and agreed with Ethan, "Sure is."

Michael struggled to get his pack out of the trunk. He had brought the three-person tent they would sleep in that night.

"Tent's heavy," Michael grunted. "Good thing I didn't bring any food. I don't know if I could carry it," he laughed.

"Alright, boys," Ethan's dad said, looking down at them seriously. "We've all camped together before. You know the rules. Leave no trace. Be smart and careful about making fire. Hang your food high from a tree branch, so that the animals can't get it. That last one is important. Don't leave anything in your packs, or you might wake up to Bigfoot stealing your food. Any questions before I go?"

"Did you say Bigfoot?" Michael asked Ethan's dad.

"Ethan, you didn't tell them?" Ethan's dad asked, looking at his son.

Ethan rolled his eyes and turned to his friends. "Grandpa and dad say that Bigfoot lives in these woods. Of course Bigfoot isn't real, so..."

"When I was your age, I was out camping with Grandpa one summer and we saw him. Just remember boys," Ethan's dad said looking at each boy in turn, "you don't bother him, and he won't bother you. Just don't leave any food in your packs, or take it into your tent. He *loves* chocolate bars."

"Dad, please. There's no such thing as Bigfoot."
Ethan looked at his friends. "He's just trying to scare us.
Go home, dad. We've got this."

"Just remember what I said," Ethan's dad said.
"Ethan, you've got your phone. Call me if you need me. I'll
be at this same spot to pick you up tomorrow at noon.
Have fun, boys."

With those last words, Ethan's dad got in the car,
started it up, and drove off.

Ethan looked at his friends. "Alright, guys, follow
me!"

Ethan's Grandpa's land was huge. It was over three
hundred acres of forest, prairie and even had a small lake.
Ethan's Grandpa had made a small campsite near that lake
and that's where Ethan was leading his friends.

There wasn't much of a trail to follow, just a narrow
dirt path that was worn down from years of booted feet
trampling on it. Trees loomed over the boys as they walked
deeper into the woods.

"Did your dad and grandpa really see a Bigfoot?"
asked Bennett.

"They say they did, but they're just messing around," Ethan huffed under the weight of his overfull pack.

"I hope they're telling the truth," Michael chimed in. "I think it'd be awesome to see a Bigfoot."

"You'd pee your pants, Michael," Bennett said with a laugh.

"Well, you'd cry if *you* saw one," Michael chided back at Bennett.

"We'll be lucky if we see a squirrel with how loud you two talk," Ethan said to his friends. "There's no such thing as Bigfoot."

"Probably not," Michael said, "but it would be cool if there were. I've read all about them. Apparently some people call them skunk apes because they smell bad like skunks."

"Fascinating," Bennett said, rolling his eyes.

"And sometimes they throw rocks at trees to scare people away," Michael continued.

"Bigfoot isn't real," Ethan repeated.

"Maybe," Michael said, "but it would be cool if he was," he said again.

A few more minutes passed before the group came to a fork in the trail.

"Which way?" Michael asked Ethan.

"Hold on. I'm thinking."

"You don't know?" Bennett asked, a bit of alarm creeping into his voice.

"I know. I just need to *think* a second," Ethan explained. "Okay, we go right. In a few more minutes we should reach a large boulder. We turn left at the boulder and then in a few more minutes we'll be at the campsite," Ethan stated confidently.

They walked for several more minutes, but never came across a boulder. Eventually Ethan stopped them again. He shrugged off his heavy pack and sat down on it, rubbing his shoulders. Maybe his dad was right. Maybe he did pack too much stuff.

"We're lost, aren't we?" Michael asked as he too removed his pack.

"We're not lost. I just need to think a minute," Ethan said.

"You said that last time before you got us lost," Michael said.

"Be quiet, both of you!" Bennett hissed.

Ethan and Michael looked at Bennett, surprised at the tone in his voice.

"Listen, I know where we're going. We just..." Ethan began.

Bennett cut him off, "Shhh, listen."

Bennett was standing stock still. He held his hand out to the other two, motioning them not to move. He cupped his ears and closed his eyes.

Off in the distance all three boys heard a soft *thunk* sound.

"What was that?" Michael asked no one in particular.

"Don't know," Bennett responded in a whisper.

"Probably the sound from the road," Ethan explained, standing back up.

"We're pretty far from the road," Bennett said.

Ethan began to respond when suddenly the same *thunk* noise sounded again, but this time closer. It sounded like something hard smashing into a tree.

"Some kind of animal, maybe?" Michael ventured a guess.

"Probably," Ethan agreed.

"I don't know..." Bennett said.

Ethan had spent a lot of his life in the woods, hiking and camping with his dad and Grandpa. He knew most of the sounds the woods made, but this sound was a mystery. It wasn't a woodpecker. It didn't shake the ground like when a tree fell. He couldn't say what was making the noise.

Even worse than the noise was the feeling of being watched. Ethan had felt eyes on him ever since they entered the woods. He felt the same way when he and his dad camped in Alaska and were followed by a grizzly bear. He thought maybe it was a coyote watching him now, or maybe a wild dog.

Again there was a loud *thunk*. This time it seemed to come from much closer.

"I think I know where we went wrong," Ethan said, in a rush of words. He was eager to get away from whatever was making that sound. "We've got to back track a little and take that other fork in the trail. Then we'll get to the campsite in no time. Come on." He stood and shouldered his pack. He headed off down the trail, back the way they came. The two other boys quickly followed.

They reached the place where the trail forked without hearing any more strange noises. They took the other path and eventually began to feel a little less nervous. They passed the large boulder, like Ethan said they would, and in a few more minutes found the campsite.

The campsite was a cleared area of land with a fire ring. There was a raised wooden platform, about a foot off the ground, where they could pitch their tent. The three boys tossed off their packs and began to set up camp. They worked together and erected the tent. Then they gathered a pile of firewood. By the time all the work had been done, the sun had begun to fall behind the trees.

"Let's get some food going," Michael said, wiping sweat from his brow.

"Yeah, good idea," Bennett agreed.

"Empty what you brought onto my pack," Ethan said.

Ethan and Bennett pooled their food supplies together while Michael just watched.

Ethan took inventory of their food. "So for dinner tonight we've got one package of dehydrated spaghetti and sauce, a can of soup, some trail mix, and beef jerky to split three ways."

"Plus s'mores stuff," Bennett added.

"Right, and s'mores stuff. I guess that'll be enough for the night," Ethan said.

Michael picked up a small rock and threw it in Ethan's general direction. Ethan dodged the rock, and it bounced off the tree with a *thunk*.

Michael looked at Ethan, and then they both looked at Bennett.

"That was it," Bennett said. "The sound we heard."

"Couldn't be," Ethan said, shaking his head. "There aren't any animals that can throw rocks in these woods."

Michael picked up a stone the size of his hand and threw it against a tree. It gave a resounding *THUNK*!

"That is *definitely* the sound. Maybe it was Bigfoot," Michael said with a laugh like he was trying to joke, but his face didn't look like he was kidding.

"Let's get a fire going," Bennett said, eyeballing the sun that was nearly hidden entirely behind the trees.

"Good idea," Michael agreed.

Ethan pulled a Ziploc baggie filled with dryer lint from his pack, put the lint in a pile of kindling and used a match to start the fire. Within moments they had a steady blaze going.

"Well, I'm not going to lie," Michael said looking out at the surrounding woods, "I'm a little creeped out right now."

"There's no such thing as Bigfoot," Ethan said while rummaging through his pack.

"What are you looking for," Bennett asked?

Ethan pulled his cellphone from a pocket. "This," he replied.

Ethan poked at the smartphone a few times and then turned it toward the fire. An old fashioned camera sound issued from the phone speaker. Ethan snapped a few more pictures of the camp and his friends in the last of the day's dying light.

"How are you so calm?" Michael asked.

"The fire looks cool, and I want a few photos from our first time camping alone," he said.

"What about the noises? I don't really believe in Bigfoot either," Bennett said, "but that rock hitting the tree sure sounded like what we heard earlier."

"Yeah, and like I said, people say Bigfoot sometimes throw rocks to scare people away," Michael added.

"Let's forget about it and eat," Ethan said as he put the soup can near the fire. "Besides there's nothing we can do about it now. We're here."

"We could go to your Grandpa's house," Bennett said.

"Or you could call your dad and ask him to pick us up," Michael added.

"No way. If we chicken out tonight, then we'll never be allowed to camp alone again," Ethan said. "All that has happened is we heard a noise and don't know where it came from. That's it. There's weird noises all the time in the woods. You both know that."

"You're right," Bennett agreed. He crossed some branches across the fire and set a small metal pot on top of them. "I'll get some water boiling for the spaghetti."

After eating dinner, the group began to toast marshmallows for the s'mores. Twice Michael set the marshmallow he was roasting on fire. Instead of blowing the fire out like anyone else, Michael frantically waved the stick around, trying to use the air to put the fire out.

"Stop waiving the stick around and just blow it out," Ethan said laughing.

Michael continued to swing the stick around, the flaming marshmallow illuminating the night around him. Suddenly, the marshmallow flew off the stick and nearly hit Bennett in the face. He was able to dive out of the way just in time. The three boys laughed so hard that Ethan fell off of the tree stump he had been sitting on.

They were still catching their breath from the laughter when they heard something crunching through the woods. Something big. Something walking on two feet.

"That sounds like some big footsteps," Michael said, suddenly springing to his feet.

"Uh, Ethan," Bennett stammered, "what do we do?"

Ethan couldn't think of any response. He was too busy staring at a large dark shadow deep in the woods that was coming their way.

Michael spotted the shadow next, "Ethan," he hissed. "It's coming this way!"

The shadow moved across the leaves hanging low on the trees.

Bennet began to move backwards and away from the approaching form.

The shadowy figure was just outside the scant light cast by the fire when it spoke.

"Ho, boys!" a voice called out. "How do?"

"Bigfoot can talk?" Michael gasped.

"That's my Grandpa, stupid," Ethan laughed, as he tried to shake the fear from his voice.

Ethan's Grandpa emerged into the firelight.

"Hi, gramps," Ethan said, giving his grandpa a hug. "Dad said you wouldn't be back until tomorrow."

"Well, that was the original plan," he said, moving closer to the fire and looking at each boy in turn, "but I wanted to get home in time to see you and your friends."

Ethan, Bennett, and Michael each smiled at each other and laughed.

"What's the joke?" Grandpa asked.

"Thought you were a Bigfoot," Michael said.

"I don't smell that bad do I?" Grandpa asked.

"What do you mean?" Bennett asked Grandpa.

"Well, its common knowledge that Bigfoots smell remarkably similar to skunks. If you thought I was a Bigfoot than either your nose isn't working or mine isn't."

"That's why some people call them skunk apes," Michael said, beaming with pride.

"That's right, young man," Grandpa agreed with Michael.

Michael looked at Ethan and Bennett with a huge smug smile on his face. "Told you so."

"Grandpa, don't encourage these guys. They're already scared enough as it is."

"Why ya'll scared?" Grandpa asked, the firelight dancing across his wrinkled face.

"We heard rocks hitting trees earlier," Michael answered.

"We don't *know* that's what we heard," Ethan said.

"It sure sounded like it," Bennett agreed with Michael.

"Rocks, huh?" Grandpa said with a frown. "That's peculiar behavior for the guy we got in these woods."

Ethan slapped his palm on his forehead. "No, grandpa. Please don't get started."

"Yeah, our boy Ethan here doesn't believe in Bigfoot," Grandpa said looking at Bennett. "He tell you that?"

"He did, sir," Bennett replied.

"He's wrong of course. Bigfoot is real. I've seen him in these very woods."

"Is he dangerous," Michael asked?

"Dangerous? I don't know. I guess he could be. He's so big and strong that I know I wouldn't make him mad. But I tell you what, in all the time I've been in these woods, he's never bothered me. In fact, I've only seen him a few times, and always just for a moment before he's gone. He's very shy. He's skittish like a rabbit. Dangerous? Nah, I don't think so."

They all watched the fire for a little while. The crackle of the burning logs and the sound of frogs in the pond were the only sounds in the night. As Grandpa stood the sound of his creaking knees joined the other night sounds.

"Well, I think I'm ready to hit the hay," Grandpa said, dusting off the seat of his pants. "You boys have a good night."

Ethan's grandpa turned to walk away, but stopped after only one step. He turned back toward the group of boys gathered around the fire.

"One thing to remember," he said, his finger pointing at each of them in turn, "Don't leave any food around your site. Creatures of all sizes might come looking for it." With that Grandpa turned and walked off into the dark woods.

"He doesn't have a flashlight," Michael said, staring off into the woods.

"Doesn't need it. He knows these woods. He's been walking them for more years than we've been alive."

"Then wouldn't you think he might know what he's talking about when he says Bigfoot lives here?" Michael asked.

"He's just telling tales," Ethan said.

"I don't know..." Bennett said.

The full moon was high in the sky, but mostly hidden by clouds. Little light made it through the thick canopy of tree limbs. The campfire flicked shadows against tree stumps and the tent. The boys huddled close around the fire and for some reason spoke only in soft voices.

"Almost out of firewood," Bennett observed.

"I think that means it's time to go to sleep," Ethan said as he stood and stretched.

The other two mumbled their agreements.

"All the food is in the food bag, right?" Ethan asked.

"Yep," Michael said.

"Yeah," added Bennett.

Ethan took the food bag and, using a rope, tied it to a high tree branch, safely out of the reach of animals. Bennett used some of his water to extinguish the fire and Michael set their packs against a tree.

Soon all three boys were laying in their sleeping bags inside the tent.

"Overall, I say this was a good first time camping alone," Ethan observed. "I can't wait for our next trip."

"Someplace that doesn't have Bigfoot," Michael said.

"Thought you wanted to see Bigfoot?" Bennett asked.

"I've changed my mind," Michael replied.

The boys quieted down. The cicadas chittered in the night, and the frogs croaked near the lake. A foul smell wafted in the air.

"Ugh," Ethan gasped, "skunk!"

"Oh, no!" Michael replied. "Bigfoot!"

Large footsteps crunched twigs and leaves in the distance. It came closer. Soon they could hear something walking around outside the tent. Something big.

Bennett was sitting up in his sleeping bag staring in the direction of the noise.

"What is it?" Bennett asked Ethan in a whisper.

Ethan put his finger to his lips in the universal sign of *be quiet*.

"Like I said, probably a skunk," Ethan whispered.

"Sounds a lot bigger than a skunk."

The creature made a deep *huff* noise, and seemed to be rustling through their packs, which they had left leaning against a tree near the tent.

"It's Bigfoot," Michael said too loudly.

The noise outside their tent stopped.

All three boys held their breath. It seemed like even the cicadas and frogs had stopped their nighttime sounds.

A strong wind had pushed the clouds clear of the night sky. Moonlight shined down through the tree canopy. A shadow spread across the wall of the tent. The shadow had a similar shape to that of a man, but much larger.

Whatever was outside the tent hefted a pack from the ground. It rummaged through it, took something out, dropped the pack and moved away.

The shadow left the side of the tent. The boys listened as the footsteps slowly moved off into the distance. After a few moments the creature was gone and the insect and frog noises normal to the woods resumed.

Ethan dared to speak and the first thing he said was, "It wasn't Bigfoot."

"How can you say that?" Michael groaned. "We just saw one!"

"We don't know what we saw."

"I have to go with Michael on this one," Bennett said.

"I bet it was my dad, or grandpa, playing a trick on us. Bet they planned this whole thing from the start."

Bennett seemed to think about it for a minute, "You think so?"

"I guarantee it," Ethan said with conviction.

"It took something from my pack" Michael said.

"How do you know it was your pack?" Ethan asked Michael.

"Well..." Michael began sheepishly.

"What?" Bennett asked.

"I think I know what it took," Michael said.

"What?" Bennett asked.

"I forgot, but I did actually bring some food. I had a peanut butter and honey sandwich leftover pizza in my pack. I forgot it was there."

Ethan groaned.

"I'm sorry! I forgot."

Bennett moved to the tent door and slowly unzipped it. He poked his head out and looked around. "Looks like whatever that thing was, it's gone now," he said.

He unzipped the door the rest of the way and then all three boys exited the tent. They went to the tree where they had placed the packs earlier. Two of the packs were there, still leaning against the tree where they were left. The third pack was a few feet away, rummaged through and pockets all open.

"That's my pack," Michael said, pointing to the one on the ground. He knelt next to it and examined the contents. "My sandwich is gone."

"Who knew Bigfoot liked peanut butter sandwiches?" Bennett asked.

"It wasn't Bigfoot," Ethan said. "Let's just go back to sleep."

The three boys went back to the tent, but Ethan was the only one who got any sleep. Bennett and Michael stayed up the rest of the night, whispering about what had happened earlier.

The next morning, the boys ate what little they had brought for breakfast and then hastily packed up the campsite. They were ready to hike to the trailhead and meet Ethan's dad when Ethan stopped them.

"Hold on guys. One last photo to celebrate our first night camping alone," Ethan said, removing his cellphone from his pants pocket. The three boys posed close together as Ethan held the phone out at arm's length and snapped a photo.

"To celebrate surviving a meeting with Bigfoot," Michael said.

They hiked back to the trailhead and met Ethan's dad there.

"Hello, fellas," Ethan's dad said in greeting. "How'd the camping go?"

"We saw him. We saw Bigfoot!" Michael shouted in reply. "He ate my sandwich."

Ethan and his friends piled into his dad's car and they began talking over each other. Michael talking about how Bigfoot ate his sandwich and Bennett talking about the rocks hitting the trees. Ethan was ignoring it all.

Ethan took out his cell phone and opened his camera app. He looked at the selfie they had taken before hiking to the trailhead. Michael looked goofy with his hair all over the place. Bennett looked tired.

There was something else in the photo, though. Something in the background of the picture. There was something behind them in the trees. It was a large shape. It looked like it could be a person, but it had to be over eight feet tall and it was very hairy.

"It can't be," Ethan whispered to himself.

But there it was. Their selfie with Bigfoot.

Triplets

By David Kobb

Being a twin wasn't as much fun as people thought. James Goodwin had been a twin his entire life and was about sick of it. His brother Quinton was about the most annoying person in the world. Wherever James went, Quinton wanted to go . Whatever James said, Quinton agreed. Whatever James did, Quinton wanted to do too. Sometimes James wished his brother were someone else.

"Wash your hands," Mrs. Goodwin said, waving a wooden ladle at him and his brother.

"Already did, mom," James said.

"Yeah, mom. Already did," Quinton joined in.

James wasn't sure he did it on purpose, but he hated how even Quinton's voice sounded just like his. James glared at his twin brother.

"Really? Did you get under the fingernails?" their mom asked with a suspicious eye.

"No," Quinton answered before James could. "We'll go wash again."

James glared at him. *If you're going to get caught in a lie*, he thought, *at least don't take me down with you.*

That was one thing that was different between James and Quinton. James could lie to his mother with a smile on his lips, but Quinton would cave. Quinton would try to lie, but when their mother pushed back, he would crack.

James and Quinton went to the bathroom to wash their hands again.

"Can't keep your mouth shut, can you?" James asked.

"I don't like lying to mom," Quinton responded.

"You're pathetic." James splashed Quinton with water as he left the bathroom. He would give anything for a different brother.

At dinner James didn't feel like dessert, so he turned down the chocolate chip cookies his mom had made. Quinton refused desert too and James knew it was only because he had turned it down first.

That night, after they had prepared for bed, Mrs. Goodwin asked them to say their prayers. She stood in their bedroom door and watched as James and Quinton kneeled next to their beds and prayed. Quinton prayed for his brother to love him, and James prayed for his brother to disappear.

James slept poorly that night. He had strange dreams about his brother crawling in and out of their bedroom window. He dreamt his brother stood over his bed and glared down at him, but it wasn't really his brother. His brother was gone.

James was shaken awake by his mother.

"Time to get up."

"Okay, mom," he said wiping the sleep from his eyes.

"Where's your brother?" she asked James.

James looked over to his brother's empty bed.

His heart began to race. Quinton was never awake before James. *Was his brother gone?* James wondered. *Did his prayers come true? Was Quinton really gone?*

Then a toilet flushed, and Quinton came out of the bathroom in his pajamas.

"Morning, mom," he said.

"Hi, sweetie. You're up early."

"Had to pee," Quinton explained.

Another night of unanswered prayers, thought James.

James asked his mother for scrambled eggs for breakfast. Quinton asked for toast.

"Toast?" Mrs. Goodwin asked. "But James is having scrambled eggs."

"I know, but I feel like toast. Is that okay?" Quinton asked, smiling at his mother.

"Of course it's okay. It's just surprising. You always want what James wants."

"Not today," Quinton said, looking at James.

James looked back at his brother. Why was Quinton asking for toast? For as long as James could remember, Quinton always asked for the same thing for breakfast. First he was up before James, and now he's asking for a different breakfast. *Something strange is going on with my brother,* James thought.

It was a Saturday and the sun was shining. James looked out the kitchen window and watched his brother kicking a soccer ball around in the back yard. Like most days he wanted to spend the day away from his brother.

"I think I'll go for a walk, mom," James said.

"Okay, take your brother with you," she insisted.

"Do I have to?" James whined.

"Yes."

"But, mom..." he pleaded, but his mother stopped him short.

"Stop. You're brothers. He loves you so much. Why can't you just show him a little love back? Is it so bad that he wants to be like you? He just wants to have a great brother, and to be a great brother. If you aren't good to him, one day you'll regret it."

James fumed, but knew his mother wouldn't change her mind. "Fine. I'll take him with me."

James went out to the backyard. "I'm going for a walk," James said, sneering at his brother. "You can come if you want."

"Okay," Quinton agreed.

Quinton insisted that they walk along the train tracks, running behind their house.

"Keep up!" James demanded as his brother fell behind.

"Slow down!"

James stopped and stared at a dead groundhog lying besides the rails. It was bloated so fat that James thought it might burst. A rock flew past James and hit the carcass. It made a sound like a snare drum. James nearly jumped out of fright.

"What are you doing?" James asked.

Quinton didn't answer right away. Instead he spent the next several seconds staring at the bloated remains of the groundhog.

"Did mom ever tell you that we're triplets? Not twins. She had three boys. Not two." Quinton slowly turned his gaze from the rotting groundhog to James.

"You're stupid," James said, not believing a word out of his twin's mouth.

"No, I'm not."

"You're stupid, *and* you're a liar."

"I'm not lying," Quinton said. "It's true. They named him Isaiah. But mom and dad knew they couldn't take care of three kids, so they put one of us in an orphanage. They chose Isaiah, but it could have been any one of us. The problem was that Isaiah was never adopted. The people running the orphanage said he was crazy because as he grew older he liked to draw pictures of dead things. Is that so bad? Eventually, they put him in an insane asylum.

Even though it was a sunny day, James began to feel cold. He didn't like the way Quinton was staring at him. It was like looking into a mirror and seeing someone else with your face in the reflection, someone crazy.

Quinton leaned in close and whispered in James' ear. "They locked him away. They locked him away. They locked him away. They locked him away. They locked him away. They locked him away. But he got out!"

A train whistle blew right at the end of Quinton's story, and James nearly jumped out of his shoes. Quinton laughed when he saw James' fear. James was ashamed for letting his brother scare him.

"It was the train," James said pointing down the tracks at the quickly approaching train.

James began to move off the tracks, but Quinton grabbed his arm and pulled him back.

"What are you doing, idiot?" James said, struggling to break free from his brother's grip. "Let go of me!"

"I don't think I will," Quinton said. He wrapped both arms around James, and they struggled on the tracks.

James twisted and turned. He tried to stomp on his brother's foot, but Quinton was able to get out of the way.

The train blew its whistle again, long and loud. It was getting closer. Quinton growled and threw James to the ground. The train's breaks screeched, but it was too late. Quinton jumped away just in time. James didn't.

Quinton stood panting besides the tracks. From the woods off to one side of the tracks a figure emerged. He walked slowly toward Quinton. Quinton turned from the tracks and looked at the figure approaching him. The boy looked just like him.

"Hello, Quinton," the boy that threw James in front of the train said to the other boy approaching from the trees.

The boy walked slowly toward the tracks as the train still tried to grind to stop. "Did you have to do that, Isaiah?" he asked.

"He was never going to be a good brother to you, Quinton," Isaiah explained.

"But did you have to do that?" Quinton waved his hand toward the dead body of their brother, tears streaming from his eyes.

"We agreed. I would pretend to be you so that I could get rid of James and take his place. You deserve a good brother, and I deserve more than the asylum. I'm going to be the best brother you could ever hope for," Isaiah said, resting his arm around Quinton's shoulders. "We're going to go for bike rides, and go camping. We're going to do all those things that James never wanted to do with you."

Quinton wiped the tears from his eyes. "You really want to go camping with me?" he asked.

"Of course I do," Isaiah said.

Quinton smiled.

Isaiah led his brother down the tracks, back toward their house. "Just remember, when we get home, call me James."

It Lives at the Bottom

By Shawn Kobb

My sister could swim like a fish. At least, that's what my parents said. Don't get me wrong. I could swim too. It's just that it involved a lot more splashing and I often ended up choking after getting half the pool up my nose.

Maddy broke the surface with her hands above her head, water spraying in all directions. In each hand was a brightly colored ring. The one in her right hand was blue and the other was red. The rings were about the same size as a Frisbee and made of rubber, but they had something heavy inside. The idea was to throw them in the pool where they'd sink to the bottom. My sister and I would take turns going after them and see who could find them both the fastest.

It was almost always Maddy.

"What was my time?" she asked as she tossed the rings to the side of the pool and pulled her swim goggles off her eyes.

I was sitting on the edge of the pool, the hot Indiana summer sun cooking my back. I grabbed the red ring and put my arm through it and spun it around like a hula hoop.

"I lost track," I said, not looking at my sister. "It seemed like a while though."

Maddy laughed and splashed water at my face and then pulled herself up to sit next to me. "Yeah, right. What was the time?"

"Twelve," I mumbled.

She laughed again. "Not bad. Well, not too bad for *me*, I guess. For *you* it would be amazing."

"Yeah, yeah. You're *so* funny. I told you, my goggles don't fit right and they slip when I go deep. Otherwise I'd be faster."

"Oh really?" Maddy asked, fake concern in her voice. "Do you want me to try adjusting them, little brother?" She reached out toward the goggles currently wrapped around my forehead.

I pulled my head back. "No, it's okay. I'm just saying. That's why."

"Maybe next time I'll just go without my goggles so it's more fair?"

I knew she was just picking on me now. Even without goggles, she'd still be faster. We both knew it. I didn't answer and kept spinning the red hoop around my forearm. It shouldn't have bothered me, but I couldn't help it. She won every single time. Yeah, she was older, but only by two years and besides...she was a *girl*.

I stood up and turned so my back was to the pool, my wet swim trunks sticking to the front of my legs. I tossed the red ring to my sister. "So are you going to throw or not?"

There was a *thunk* sound quickly followed by another as the two rubber rings hit the pool and sunk to the bottom.

"Three...two..." My sister started the countdown slowly and I tensed up, determined to jump in and find the rings quicker than ever. "One! Go!"

I whipped myself around and took a fraction of a section to look down at the water. I thought I saw the red one on the ramp that led from the shallow to the deep end.

I didn't notice the blue one, but it was always harder to spot. I'd find it after the red one. I leapt toward the spot I saw the red ring.

I kept one hand on my goggles to keep them stuck to my eyes and pinched my nose shut with my other hand. The water was cold, but with the scorching summer temperature, I welcomed the relief.

Once underwater I turned around until I could spot the red ring. It was right where I thought I'd seen it. I scooped at the water with my hands and gave a strong kick with my legs and shot over that direction. Since it was on the ramp and not all the way in the deep end, it was simple for me to grab it off the bottom of the pool. I wondered if Maddy was going easy on me. Usually we threw both rings in the deep end. Maybe she was just trying to catch me off guard.

Still underwater, I turned toward the deep end and hunted for the blue ring. After a moment, I spotted it. It was right in the center of the deep end, next to the drain that sucked the water out before pumping it back in higher up in the pool.

I knew I'd never get all the way down there on this breath. I pushed off the ramp with my feet and shot to the surface. I gulped down a huge breath of air. There was just enough time for me to hear Maddy counting out loud.

"Seven...eight..."

How in the world was I already at eight? I'd never beat her last time of twelve. Her best time was seven and mine was eleven, done only once when both rings had been lying right next to each other.

I tried to push the time out of my mind and dove back under the surface of the water. I kicked hard toward the bottom of the deep end, trying to force my body to sink down although it wanted to float up.

As I approached the blue ring, I reached forward with both hands. My depth perception was off and I missed with my left hand. My right hand managed to grab on to the plastic grate that covered the drain. Our mom told us we needed to stay away from the drain. She was worried we'd get stuck to it and drown. Maddy just laughed, but I was pretty sure Mom was serious about it.

This time though, I was glad I grabbed it because I could hold on to it and stay at the bottom easier. I poked my fingers through the holes and held on and then using my left hand reached out and grabbed the blue ring.

I pulled my feet under me, ready to make a hard push off the bottom and shoot up to the surface. I knew I had to be past twelve now, but I didn't think my time was too bad.

I kicked my feet, but instead of going up, I almost screamed in pain before remembering I was underwater. My fingers were somehow stuck on the drain. I relaxed them, but they weren't coming free.

Mom was right! The suction had me. I was going to drown!

I dropped the blue ring and bent down and grabbed at my right arm with my left hand and got my feet underneath me. I was running out of air. I had to get my hand loose quick.

I pulled and pulled. I couldn't tell why my hand wasn't coming free. The holes in the drain were definitely big enough for my fingers to slip through. It almost felt like something on the other side of the drain was holding onto to me.

I bent closer to try and look, my lungs almost exploding in my chest. I had held my breath much longer than this, but with my panic and struggling, I was using up all my oxygen fast. I had to get up. Would Maddy realize something was wrong and come help?

I lowered my face close to the drain, trying desperately to see what my fingers were stuck on. I couldn't see anything.

My feet on either side of the drain, my left hand wrapped around my right wrist, I pushed with my legs as hard as I could. With a pop I could hear underwater, my hand came free.

Just before I started to shoot up to the top of the pool and to the fresh air I needed so bad, I looked down at the drain again.

There was an eye looking at me from the other side. It was yellow with little red veins going across it and a long black pupil like our cat had. I thought...I *knew* my mind had to be playing a trick on me. There couldn't be an eye. Nothing could live under the drain. Then it blinked. One slow, lazy blink. I saw the green scaly eyelid close over the yellow eye before lifting back up to allow that strange black slit to stare at me once again.

Next thing I knew, I broke the surface of the water, coughing and gasping.

"Sixteen!" Maddy called out. "That's slow even for you. What in the..."

My sister's voice stopped its playful taunting once she realized something was wrong. She jumped in the pool and swam over to me and helped me get to the side. I grabbed on to the edge of the pool, my chest heaving.

"At...the...bottom..." I gasped out the words while my sister held on to my arm. "I saw it."

"You saw what?" She turned and peered down through the water to the blue and white tiled bottom of the pool.

I shook my head. "Something. A monster."

Maddy turned her attention away from the pool and back to me. For a moment she just stared and then she burst out laughing.

"A monster? Right..." She grabbed the red ring from my hand. "Just because you can't beat my time, you think its funny to pretend to drown?"

She didn't believe me! "I'm serious, Maddy. We have to get out of the pool and tell Mom and Dad." I started to pull myself over the edge, but she pulled me back in.

"Oh no you don't. Not so fast."

"Maddy! I mean it. There's something on the other side of the drain. I saw it. It *looked* at me. It grabbed my hand."

Now she laughed even louder. "On the other side of the drain? There's nothing on the other side of the drain except the pump. There's not even any space back there for something to live."

"There was an eye! And something grabbed my fingers." I held up my hand for her to see, but to be honest it was tough to make out any kind of scratches. My fingers hurt, but there weren't any marks there.

This time I did pull myself out of the pool. Maddy didn't try and stop me. I stood on the edge looking down at her. "I'm not joking. We have to get Dad."

She laughed again. "I tell you what. You go get Dad. I'm going to go down and take a look."

A shiver ran up my spine. "You can't go down there. You have to get out of the pool." I bent over and tried to grab her, but she kicked away from the edge and started to tread water in the middle of the deep end.

"Nice try. You've got to be quicker than that if you..."

I didn't hear the rest of what she said. I was staring at the bottom of the pool. There was a shadow. Something was coming out of the drain. At first it was long and slender like a snake, but once it cleared the small hole of the drain, it uncurled some sort of wings, but with clawed fingers at the tips like a bat. It started doing lazy circles at the bottom of the deep end of the pool.

I pointed down and tried to scream, but no words came out of my mouth.

"Ooh...I'm so scared," Maddy's voice continued to taunt. She didn't even look down. The thing swam just below her feet. Couldn't she feel it?

"Maddy," I finally managed to choke her name out. "Maddy, get out of the pool!"

I screamed the last part and finally it sank in to my sister that I wasn't joking. She scanned the water and spun herself around so that she faced the deep end. She saw the monster circling below her feet.

My sister started thrashing in the water frantically and screamed. "Stevie! Help me!" She started swimming toward me, desperately trying to reach the edge of the pool.

The creature noticed its victim trying to escape. It turned its head toward her and once again I saw that terrible yellow eye. There was only one, like the Cyclops I read about in my mythology book. The eye was in the middle of its tiny little head and beneath opened a mouth incredibly wide to reveal row after row of small needle-like teeth.

"Faster, Maddy! Faster!"

My sister was almost to the edge of the pool and I kneeled down and reached out my hands to grab her. The monster darted quickly through the water and reached out with its weird little clawed wings and wrapped them around her leg.

"It's got me, Stevie!"

I managed to grab on to one of her arms and then the other arm and pulled with all of my might. The creature was pulling in the other direction and we played tug of war with my sister. I was sure I was going to be pulled into the pool as well. I could feel my shins getting scraped along the rough stone that surrounded the edge of the pool, but I didn't let go. I pulled and I pulled.

Maddy gave a final hard kick with the foot the monster didn't have a hold of and hit the thing right in the middle of its giant, yellow eye. From my perch above I saw the eyeball squish and burst, yellow and white fluid leaking out into the clear water of our pool.

The monster screamed under water. I think I felt the sound as much as I heard it. The noise was high pitched and terrible. The monster let go of Maddy's leg and swam around in fast, erratic circles before suddenly darting back toward the drain. It pulled in its wings, turning once more into a snake, and slithered into the drain and disappeared.

I pulled Maddy up over the edge of the pool and she collapsed, panting and coughing. I flopped on to my back on the ground and stared into the sky.

My parents came out a few minutes later to find us still laying by the edge of the pool staring into the sky.

I looked up to see my dad looking down at me.

He gave a toothy grin and then suddenly scooped me up into his strong arms. "It looks like someone needs some help getting into the pool."

As I was flying into the air toward the water, I thought I saw a shadow circling at the bottom of the pool.

I heard my sister scream.

"Dad! No!"

Little Miss Toughie Tough

By David Kobb

Mika stood next to a Halloween pumpkin on the front porch, and ignored what her mother was saying to her. She tried to make her face an imitation of the scowl carved into the pumpkin when she looked up at her mom.

"I'm almost 12 and a half," Mika pleaded, "I can stay home alone."

"You turned 12 just three weeks ago. That's not really 12 and a half," Mrs. Collins said looking down at Mika.

Mr. Collins, Mika's dad, put his hand on Mika's shoulder. "In another couple of years, then   can stay home alone. Tonight, you're going to your grandma's."

"But its Halloween," Mika wailed, "I want to go trick-or-treating."

"Grandma will take you around her neighborhood," Mrs. Collins said calmly.

"Grandma lives a billion miles from anyone. I'll be able to hit like two houses before she takes me back home. Why can't Oliver watch me?" Mika asked her parents, thinking that at least if her older brother watched her, she could go trick-or-treating around their neighborhood.

"Your brother is going to a party tonight. He won't be back until late.," Mr. Collins said while looking at his watch.

"It's not fair you let him do whatever he wants," Mika said, changing her argument tactics.

"Your brother's 16. That's a lot older than 12."

"Nearly 12 and a half," Mika insisted. "You know he's going to do something stupid tonight anyways, like egg houses or ding dong ditch."

"That's besides the point," Mr. Collins said.

"You're going to let Oliver go to an unsupervised party at Brad's house, but you won't let me stay home alone and trick-or-treat just around the neighborhood. I won't even go too far. Just around the block, I promise."

"We're taking you to your grandma's. That's final," Mrs. Collins said, crossing her arms.

Just then the front door of the house opened and Mika's older brother emerged out onto the front porch.

"What are you guys still doing here?" Oliver asked his parents.

"Mika wants to stay home alone."

"You let him stay home alone when he was my age," Mika said pointing her finger in her older brother's face.

"He's a boy," Mr. Collins said, as if that explained everything.

"So? Why does it matter?"

"It just does, Toughie," Mrs. Collins said, using the nickname Mika's family had for her. The full nickname was Little Miss Toughie Tough, but usually they just called her Toughie.

"Boys are different, Toughie," her dad said with a sad smile.

Oliver chimed in, "She doesn't have to go to grandma's house. I can watch her. Brad's parents found out about the party and he had to cancel it."

"I thought you said that Brad's parents were going to be at the party," Mr. Collins said frowning at Oliver.

Since her brother was coming to her aid, Mika decided to come to his. She jumped in before Oliver could make up some lie and get himself in trouble. "So, I can stay home and go trick-or-treating?"

Her parents exchanged a look and her mom nodded once to her dad. Mika knew what that meant.

She jumped and punched her fist into the air and whooped in joy!

"You go around with her when she trick-or-treats," Mrs. Collins said to Oliver.

"Sure, mom," Oliver said, looking off into the distance like he wasn't paying attention.

"I mean it, Oliver. You go with her."

"Sheesh, ma, I said I would," he said.

Mr. Collins checked his watch again, "We're going to be late. We've got to go."

"We'll be back around midnight," their mom said. "Toughie, you do what your brother says," and then she pointed at Oliver, "and you watch out for your sister."

With that last instruction Mr. and Mrs. Collins walked to the car, waved goodbye and drove off.

"Thanks, bro," Mika said.

Oliver didn't respond. He was staring intently off into the distance. Mika followed his gaze across the street.

"What are you looking at," she asked him?

He pointed at a neighboring house . "That creepy decoration on the Feldman's porch."

Mika followed his finger and saw what he was talking about.

Their neighbors across the street, the Feldmans, always had some terrific decorations for holidays, and this Halloween was no different. Sitting in a rocking chair was some sort of monster. It wasn't like any monster Mika had ever seen though. It had dark blue skin, and three ridged horns on its head. It's fingers ended in sharp looking claws. It was terrifying. Mika loved it.

"Yeah, that's a good Halloween decoration," Mika said. "Almost looks like it could be real, doesn't it?" she asked with a smile.

"It does look pretty real," Oliver agreed. He continued to stare at it.

Mika sighed. "What is your problem?"

"I thought I saw it move."

"It's in a rocking chair, dummy, it probably moved because of the wind.

A strong wind had picked up. Orange and red leaves skittered down the street making noises like skeleton fingers scraping the inside of a coffin.

"I think it's going to storm tonight," Oliver said taking a look at the dark clouds gathering in the sky."

"Just as long as it holds off until after I'm done trick-or-treating," Mika said. "Speaking of which," she nudged her brother in the ribs, "Let's go soon."

The sun still blazed on the horizon, but was quickly falling behind a growth of trees at the end of the street.

"You better go change into your costume," her brother said. "We'll go as soon as it's dark. What are you going as this year?"

"Rugby player," she answered with a grin.

"But you play hockey," Oliver said with a puzzled frown.

"Yeah, but I want to play rugby now. It's tougher."

Mika was in her bedroom putting her costume on when she heard her brother holler from downstairs.

"What in the world!"

"What is it?" Mika yelled, poking her head out of her bedroom so she could be heard downstairs where Oliver was.

"Come here," he cried back to her.

Mika gave herself a once over in the mirror that hung on her closet door. She looked good, like a real rugby player. She had on a uniform and had given herself some fake bruises to complement her real ones. Satisfied with her costume, she ran downstairs.

She found Oliver staring out of a living room window. He was looking across the street again.

"What is it?" she asked, also looking across the street.

"Look at that monster decoration thing," he said.

She looked, but didn't see what the problem was. "Yeah, so?"

"Look at its arms."

"What about them?"

"They're crossed. They weren't crossed earlier."

"Weren't they?"

"No," he replied.

She studied the creature carefully. The rocking chair in which it sat was moving gently. She glanced at the tree branches in the front yard – they weren't moving. It seems the wind had died down. The house had become oddly quiet. She turned to look at her brother, but he was gone.

"Oliver? Where did you go?"

She moved away from the window, giving the creepy decoration one last look. She walked toward the kitchen in the back of the house. As she passed her parent's bedroom the door burst open and out jumped a crazy looking clown.

The clown yelled, "Hello, child, are you scared?" in a high-pitched whine.

"Nice costume, Oliver," Mika said rolling her eyes.

"Ugh!" Oliver grunted. "One day I *will* scare you."

"Not likely," Mika said with a smirk.

"Oh right, you're Little Miss Toughie Tough, I forgot. You ready to go trick-or-treating, Toughie?"

"Yes!" she whooped.

Mika used an old pillow case to carry her candy. By the time she and Oliver had turned back onto their street, she had to use both hands to carry it.

"Only one house left to hit," Mika said to her brother.

"Where?"

"The Feldman's house. I want to see that creepy monster decoration up close."

As they walked toward their neighbors house Mika stopped.

"What is it," asked Oliver?

"Look," Mika said pointing toward the Feldman house. "It's gone."

She was right. The rocking chair on the Feldman's front porch sat empty. The spooky monster, whatever it might be, was gone.

"They must have run out of candy," Oliver said.

"No way," "Not the Feldmans. Their porch light is still on. Let's go talk to them."

"Let's just go home," Oliver said, his voice uneven.

"You can if you want," Mika said. "I'll be home after I talk to Mr. or Mrs. Feldman."

"Fine, but you come straight home after. I don't want to get in trouble if someone kidnaps you."

Mika rolled her eyes. "Our house is right across the street. I'll be home in two minutes."

Oliver walked home as Mika walked up the porch steps of the Feldman's house. She rang the doorbell. After just a moment the door opened and Mrs. Feldman looked down at Mika.

"Trick-or-treat!" Mika said.

"Oh, look at all of those bruises," Mrs. Feldman said. She poked at a bruise on Mika's arm.

Mika winced, "That's one's real, Mrs. F."

A pained look crossed Mrs. Feldman's face, "Oops. Sorry, Mika. Here you go." She dropped two handfuls of candy into Mika's bag.

"Thanks, Mrs. F," Mika said.

"Well, have a spooky night," Mrs. Feldman said followed by her best witches cackle. She began to shut the door.

"Wait! One second, Mrs. F. I have a quick question."

"Sure, Mika. What is it?"

"What happened to that decoration you had on the rocking chair earlier tonight? It's gone now."

Mrs. Feldman looked over at the empty rocking chair and then back at Mika. "Mika, we never had a decoration in that chair."

"I saw it earlier," Mika said. "It had blue skin and three great big horns. It's hands ended in sharp looking claws. It was wearing a black cloak..."

Mrs. Feldman was looking down at Mika with a confused expression. Then she grinned. "Oh, that's good, Mika. That's really good. You had me going for a second. You almost gave me the chills. To imagine some monster on my front porch that I didn't put there – yikes!" Then Mrs. Feldman really did shiver.

"So, you really didn't have a monster decoration in the chair," Mika asked?

"Oh, you're cruel, Mika," Mrs. Feldman said with a smile. "I liked your description of it though. Maybe next year I really will make a monster decoration like that. Well...goodnight, Mika."

Mrs. Feldman closed the door and left Mika standing alone on the front porch. After a moment, the porch light turned off. Mika headed home.

Mika opened the front door to her house. "I asked Mrs. F about that decoration, but she said..." Mika realized she was talking to herself. Oliver wasn't in the living room.

She walked to his bedroom door and knocked. No answer.

"Oliver!" she yelled. The house was quiet. Empty.

She was going to check the basement, but stopped when she noticed a note on the dining room table. She read it. It was from Oliver. He said that he got a call from Brad and that the party was back on. He would be back before their parents got home. He'd get her ice cream on his way home if she promised not to tell their parents he left.

Mika put the note down and looked around the big empty house. She was home alone on Halloween. She let out a squeak of joy and ran around the kitchen. She didn't care what her brother said, she was going to tell her parents that she was left alone. She'd been left alone and she was just fine. Then maybe they would let her stay home alone whenever.

She stopped running around the kitchen and paused to catch her breath. What should she do with her first night home alone? It was Halloween after all. How about a scary movie and popcorn?

Out in the living room she turned on the television and scrolled through the family's collection of movies. She found just the right scary movie, called <u>It's In the House</u> and hit play. She sat in the big recliner that her dad always claimed, and wiggled deep into the cushions to get comfy. She turned off the table lamp next to the chair and the house was suddenly illuminated only by the glow of the television.

A few minutes into the movie there was a knock on the front door. Mika hit pause and listened. There was another knock. She decided it was probably some trick-or-treaters out late and ignored it. She didn't have any candy to hand out except her own and that definitely wasn't going to happen. She resumed the movie.

Popcorn! She had forgotten to make popcorn. She paused the movie again and went out into the kitchen. She turned on the light, found a bag of microwave popcorn, tossed it into the microwave and then walked back to the living room.

The front door was open. Mika paused in between the kitchen and the living room. She stared at the front door. Maybe Oliver or her parents had come home early. The light from the kitchen and the glow from the television cast shadows on the walls. Mika crept toward the front door and then shut it.

"Oliver!" she yelled.

Silence.

"Mom? Dad?"

No response.

She made her way upstairs as quietly as she could. She would get her hockey stick and her cellphone from her bedroom. At the top of the stairs she paused and listened. She didn't hear anything other than the wind that had picked up again outside.

She walked to her bedroom. The door was closed, but she remembered leaving it open earlier. She opened the door and turned on the light. She grabbed her hockey stick, resting near the door, and walked to her bed to grab her cell phone. She dialed her brother's number.

The phone range twice before he answered. She could hear music in the background.

"Oliver?" she asked.

"What do you want?"

"Are you at home?"

"No, didn't you see my note?"

"Yeah," she answered. She moved to close her bedroom door and locked it. "It's just..."

"Is something wrong," he asked?

She didn't want to tell him about the front door being opened. She might cost herself her chance at being able to stay home alone.

"No, nothing's wrong. I just wanted to make sure you weren't home."

"I'll be home around 11:00," he said. "Promise you won't tell mom and dad that I left?"

"As long as the next time I want to stay home alone you get my back."

"Deal," Oliver said.

"Okay, have fun at the party. Bye."

She ended the call and looked around her room. This wasn't like her, hiding in her room from nothing. She was tougher than this.

She gripped her hockey stick firmly and swung open her bedroom door. She walked downstairs and back into the living room. The front door was still shut. She sat back down in her dad's favorite chair and turned the movie back on.

After a few minutes she remembered that there was popcorn in the microwave and went to get it. When she came back to the living room, the front door was open again. She took her hockey stick to the open door and peered outside. Her front yard was empty and all the trick-or-treaters had gone home to eat their candy.

She closed the door and turned around. There, standing a few feet from her was the three-horned monster. It made a huffing noise and began to walk toward her.

For a moment Mika stood motionless. Her mouth hung open as she stared at the creature's three horns and scaly skin. She couldn't move.

The creature walked even closer. It moved closer and closer until it was so close that it reached out with its sharp talons and grabbed at her.

Mika's reflexes took over and before she realized what she was doing she used a Jiu-Jitsu move she learned in her previous lesson and knocked the monster to the ground. As it hit the floor it let out a very human sounding groan. She didn't care. She took her hockey stick and began to swing at the creature's head when she heard it speak.

"No! Stop!"

She heard steps thumping down the stairs and turned to look at the new threat. It was a creepy clown. She almost swung the stick at the clown before she stopped herself.

"Oliver?" she asked in confusion.

"Toughie, stop!" he yelled.

Oliver walked over to the monster, still groaning on the ground, and held out a hand. The monster took it and was helped to his feet. It removed its mask and Mika saw that it was Oliver's friend Brad.

"What's going on?" Mika asked.

"Holy cow, your sister's scary," Brad said to Oliver.

"Yeah, she's tough alright," Oliver replied. Then he turned to Mika. "Admit it, you were scared a little bit."

Mika realized the whole thing was a set up. Oliver and Brad had teamed up to try and scare her.

"I wasn't scared at all," Mika said as she sat back down in the comfy recliner, ate a handful of popcorn and resumed the movie.

The Silver Brush

By Shawn Kobb

"No!"

I awoke instantly, but confused. Had I been dreaming? Did I yell out in my sleep? It was the middle of the night, but the full moon shining through my bedroom window made it easy enough to see.

I touched the bed between my legs and was relieved to find the sheets dry. I hadn't had an accident in almost two years, but I still worried about wetting the bed. I saw a hunched figure sitting on the other bed. My breath caught in my throat and I almost yelled for my parents before I remembered.

"Megan?" I whispered. "What are you doing?"

My cousin looked over at me, her eyes glistened in the moonlight like she had been crying. Her tears made me really uncomfortable. I wasn't very happy to be sharing my room with my cousin -- my <u>girl</u> cousin at that. If she was going to cry as well, I didn't think I could take it.

For a second Megan didn't respond and then she jerked as though startled. She blinked her eyes and made a big sigh.

"Nothing. Only a bad dream."

I would rather have died than admit to anyone that I thought Megan was the prettiest girl I had ever seen, but the way she talked was the best thing about her. She sounded like she was from a movie where the guys carried swords and pirates were always capturing the girls.

Megan was staying with us for almost ten days this summer. She came from a small town in Ireland and the plan was that maybe I would stay there next year. My parents thought I didn't know, but I heard them whispering about her. I knew Megan's trip was more than a vacation. She had problems back home.

She wiped her eyes, but neither of us said anything about it. We had met a few times before this visit, but didn't know each other that well yet. Our parents liked to talk about how close we were as kids, but since neither of us really remembered that far back, it didn't help much.

I thought she wanted to talk, but I wanted to go back to sleep. "Okay. I'm going back to bed."

I turned under the blankets away from her. I felt like she was staring into the back of my head, but I refused to turn around. I didn't know what you were supposed to say to a girl who had a nightmare. I would probably say the wrong thing and make it worse.

After a few minutes I heard her move and whisper goodnight. I pretended to be asleep.

The next thing I knew, the bright morning sun had replaced the full moon. I rubbed my face and checked the bed next to mine, but it was empty except for a pile of sheets and blankets. Megan must have already gone to breakfast. My parents had planned something for almost every day Megan was here. Some things were cool, like going to Six Flags and riding the rollercoasters, but other days we just had things like museums.

I started to get dressed and then remembered at the last second to lock my door. I never had to do that before, but I didn't want my cousin walking in right when I was pulling on my blue jeans. Looking at myself in the mirror, my hair was wild like I had spent the night sleeping in the middle of a tornado. I tried to mush it into place with my hands, but that only seemed to make matters worse. I grabbed for the comb I kept on top of my dresser, but couldn't find it. In its place was a large, fancy brush.

The handle and back of the brush was metal. I think it was real silver because it had the little black spots that got on my mom's fancy tea set. The bristles were thick and rough and I was sure they could tame any hair. I hadn't seen Megan use the brush, but she must have brought it with her.

With a shrug, I decided to give the brush a shot and pulled it through my stubborn hair. After a few seconds I decided I looked as good as I was going to and put the brush back where I found it and left my room hoping to find some bacon and eggs.

As I suspected, Megan sat at the table eating with my mom. Dad stood at the stove frying up more bacon. He ate as much as he put on the plate next to him. I grabbed a plate and helped myself.

"Hey there, sleeping beauty," my dad said and rubbed my head.

I felt blushed and quickly moved out of reach, shooting a quick glance over at Megan. I noticed my mom smirk, but my cousin didn't seem to pay any attention. In fact, she barely seemed to know where she was. She stared straight ahead, chewing a mouthful of eggs slowly.

I saw down and started eating.

"How'd you sleep, Megan?" my mom asked.

My cousin gave a little shrug. "Okay, I guess." Her red eyes told a different story.

"I imagine you still have a bit of jet lag," Mom said. I didn't really understand what jet lag was, but it was seemed to be some sort of disease you got when flying. Mom said we had it too a few years ago when we went to visit family in Ireland.

"Yeah," Megan said quietly.

Sensing that Megan wasn't in the mood to talk this morning, my parents turned their attention on me. "And how about you?"

"How about me what?" I said around a mouthful of bacon.

Dad sat at the table with us. "How did you sleep? And don't talk with your mouth full."

I finished my bite before answering. "Fine." I figured there wasn't any reason to embarrass Megan by telling them she woke me up with her nightmare.

Mom and Dad smiled at each other. "What amazing conversation we're having this morning," Mom said. "Maybe eventually we'll move past one word answers?"

"Yeah," Dad said, and we all laughed. Except Megan.

Mom reached over and tried to smooth down my hair. I shook her hand off while avoiding looking at Megan. It was so embarrassing. "Mom, stop it."

"Well, if you would comb your hair I wouldn't have to."

"I did. I brushed it right before I came out here."

"You *brushed* your hair? Since when do you have a brush?"

I felt my cheeks burn and glanced over at my cousin across the table. Was she angry? Actually, she looked scared.

I decided to play dumb. "I used that new one you got for me."

"I didn't buy you a brush." Mom looked over at Megan. "He probably used your brush by mistake."

Megan already had pretty fair skin, but what little color she did have had all drained away. She turned as white as a ghost. I knew I had done something wrong, but I didn't get the big deal. It was only a stupid brush. It wasn't like I had lice or anything.

"I guess so," I said and then followed up with a mumbled apology to my cousin. "I'm sorry I used your brush."

For a moment, Megan didn't say anything. How could she be this mad?

"What did it look like?" She practically whispered at first, but then repeated it louder. "What did the brush look like?"

I looked to my mom and dad. Even they were confused.

"Um, big and silver and --"

Before I could even finish Megan suddenly shot up from her chair. Her eyes were wide and I was afraid she was going to cry. With a half sob and half shout, she suddenly ran from the kitchen table toward the bedroom we were sharing.

"Well," Dad said slowly. "That was weird."

"Dan," Mom said in that tone she used whenever he said something of which she didn't approve. She then looked at me. "I think you need to apologize to her."

"It's just a stupid brush! And I did say I was sorry."

Mom put a hand on my shoulder. "I don't think it's the brush. Megan's had a hard time at home lately. That's why she came to visit. I don't know what the real problem is, but she's obviously upset. So be a good cousin and go check on her."

I sighed loudly to let her know what I thought of that, but pushed my chair away from the table. I grabbed some bacon and shoved it in my mouth before walking to my room.

When I got there, the door was mostly closed, but still open a crack. I heard Megan crying inside. *Great*, I thought. *Now I get to deal with a crying girl.*

I pushed the door open a bit further and peeked in. Megan sat on the edge of her bed with her face in her hands. I hunted through the junk on top of my dresser, but the brush wasn't there. She must have put it away.

I stood awkwardly for a second thinking about what to do. Should I put my hand on her shoulder or make a joke or something? Instead, I decided to keep it simple and get it over with.

I sat on my bed and picked at the sheet without looking at her. "I'm sorry I used your brush," I mumbled.

She didn't say anything at first. *Oh great,* I thought. *Now I made it even worse. Why are girls so weird?*

"I didn't think you'd get so upset," I said. "It was only a brush and my hair was so--"

"It's not my brush."

"--messy and I thought that... Wait. What did you say?"

Megan looked up at me, her eyes still red from crying. She didn't look sad or angry. She was scared. Terrified. "That wasn't my brush. I didn't bring it with me. I came here to get away from it."

That didn't make any sense at all. "Of course you brought it. I don't own a brush. What did you do with it, anyway?"

"I didn't do anything with it." She turned away from me and it seemed like she was about to cry again. "You won't understand."

For a few seconds neither of us said anything. She was right. I didn't understand. She was talking like a crazy person. It wasn't her brush? She didn't do anything with it? That was obviously not true. I knew it wasn't mine and now it wasn't on the dresser. I finally told her as much.

Megan made a big sigh and then got up suddenly and closed the door. She came back and sat down on her bed and stared at me.

"You promise you won't think I'm crazy?"

I was afraid I already thought she might be, but she was looking at me so seriously, that I nodded. "I promise."

"I know what I'm going to tell you sounds insane, but you have to believe me. It's really important, okay?"

"Just tell me already!" She was making me really nervous. How could brushing my hair have become such a big deal?

Megan took in another big breath and then held it for a second, her shoulders tense and her eyes closed. She released the air from her lungs and then opened her eyes.

"Have you ever heard of a *banshee*?"

The word sounded very exotic, like something from China or the name of a character in one of my Japanese manga comics.

I shook my head.

"It's a Gaelic word. That's a language that some people in Ireland speak."

"What's it mean?" I asked.

Megan picked at a loose thread on the bedspread in front of her. "I don't know what it means exactly, but I know what it is."

She didn't say anything after that. I could tell she didn't want to tell me. "And?"

Finally she looked up at me, her eyes glistened like she was close to crying again. "It's a ghost."

With her funny accent, I thought I must have misunderstood her. "A what?"

"A ghost," Megan said forcefully. "A spirit. And the brush belongs to her. And you shouldn't have touched it."

I felt my jaw drop open. Was she serious? She couldn't be serious. I thought because Megan was from Ireland sometimes I didn't get her jokes. Finally, I laughed.

"Nice try," I said. "Very funny."

She maintained the same serious expression. I felt like something was really wrong. She didn't say anything at first and waited for me to finish laughing.

"I thought the same thing at first," Megan said. "When I touched the brush."

"This isn't funny, Megan. Are you trying to get me in trouble somehow?"

She shook her head. "I didn't mean for this to happen. I agreed to come here to get away from this. I never thought she would follow me."

"She? Who?"

Megan jumped to her feet. "The ghost! She followed me here. I thought I left her in Ireland, but if you saw her brush--"

"You saw it too," I interrupted. "The brush was on the dresser, but now it is gone. What did you do with it?"

Megan sat back down. Her shoulders hung and she ran a hand through her hair. "I haven't seen it here. I didn't touch it. *She* took it back. That's what she does. She leaves it out and if someone touches it, someone uses it..."

I waited for her to finish the sentence. Something told me I didn't want to know, but I had to. "What? What happens?"

"Bad things." She said it quietly, almost a whisper.

I felt all of the little hairs on the back of my neck stand up. I wanted to tell my parents, but I wasn't a little kid anymore. Besides, what would I tell them? My cousin says I'm in trouble because I used a ghost's brush? This was crazy. She was crazy.

"I'm sorry," she said. "There isn't much you can do. She will come back. And she is going to be very angry. You'll hear her first. That's how it is with a *banshee*. You hear her crying and it will get closer and closer and you won't be able to get away from it."

"Stop it!" I yelled. "It's not funny anymore." I got to my feet and started toward the door, unsure where I was going or what I was going to do.

"I'm not joking. I wish I were. I'm really sorry. I didn't mean for this to happen."

I could tell by the sound of her voice she was serious. Maybe she really was crazy? I turned back toward her and saw her standing next to my bed, tears coming from her eyes.

"What is she going to do?" I said it quietly, almost a whisper. I felt like I already knew the answer, but I wanted to hear her say it.

Megan sat back down and I joined her. "In Ireland they say that once you hear the cry of the *banshee*, death is coming."

I felt cold all over and struggled to breathe. "If I hear her cry tonight, it means I'm going to die? That's what you're saying?"

Megan shifted uncomfortably. "*Someone* is going to die."

"Wait," I said, suddenly having a thought. "But you heard her, right? You touched the brush too. You're still here."

"I'm really sorry, but--"

I wasn't about to let her squirm her way out of answering my question. "What aren't you telling me? You know something else. If you heard the *banshee*, if you touched her brush, then why are you here? Why didn't you die?" It felt mean when I said it that way. I didn't want her to die, of course, but I had to know.

Great big tears started to well up in Megan's eyes. She stared right through me as though remembering something in the past. After a few seconds, she sniffed and wiped her eyes.

"When the *banshee* cries, someone has to die. That's how it works. Almost always the person that hears her."

"*Almost* always," I said, "but not always. What about the other times?"

At first I thought she wouldn't answer. I wasn't sure what I would do if she refused to tell me. Call my parents? Tell them what she said? They would never believe me. Even I wasn't sure if I believed all this, but Megan seemed so confident. Finally, my cousin started talking again.

"Back home I had a friend," she said. "Her name was Shannon O'Brien. We weren't just friends, we were *best* friends. A lot of people thought we were sisters we were together so much."

"Megan! I don't want to hear about--" She kept talking as though I hadn't interrupted her at all.

"I can't remember a time when I didn't know Shannon. My mum told me we were even in the hospitals as babies at the same time. Our birthdays were only two days apart. I told Shannon everything. Every secret. Every dream."

She paused, remembering her friend. I didn't say anything this time. I could tell she was going somewhere with the story. I waited for her to continue.

"When Shannon..." Megan choked back a sob, but then pulled herself together. "When Shannon died, my heart broke. Everyone knew how close we were. Nobody knew what to say. I didn't talk to anyone for a week. I stopped doing my schoolwork. My parents didn't have any idea what to do. Finally, my mum talked to her cousin." Megan looked me in the eyes now. I knew our mothers were cousins. It made Megan and me second cousins.

"So you came to visit us?" I finished for her. I still didn't understand what it had to do with anything.

She nodded. "My parents thought it would be good to get away from Ireland, from all those memories for a little while. I wasn't so sure, but at first it did seem like it might help. But now..."

Megan took a big breath to stop the tears from returning. "But she followed me. She followed me here."

"Shannon? I don't understand..." I didn't want to say it, but did she think the ghost--the *banshee*--was her friend?

Megan shook her head. When she spoke next it was a whisper. She talked so quietly I had to lean in to hear her. "Not Shannon. The *banshee*. She killed Shannon. She killed Shannon because I was afraid and Shannon wasn't. Shannon died instead of me."

It was crazy. My cousin had gone nuts. But if that was true, why was I so terrified? Why did it feel like I couldn't catch my breath? I wanted to run to my parents, but I knew they would never believe me. If this was real, it was up to Megan and I to deal with it.

"So...what happened?" I asked. "Shannon found the brush? She heard the *banshee* cry?" The word sounded so foreign.

Megan looked into the distance, remembering what had happened to her friend. "No. It was me." He words were still quiet. It sounded like she was talking to herself. "We were playing in the woods near my house and I found the brush lying on the ground near a little stream. It was so pretty. I wasn't trying to do anything wrong."

She paused, but I waited for her to continue.

"I didn't tell Shannon about it at first. I don't know why. I wanted it for myself. There was something about it. It wasn't until later in the evening when I heard that terrible crying, the moaning, that we talked about it. Shannon said she couldn't hear the crying and I thought she was lying. I thought she was making fun of me and we argued. Eventually I realized she was telling the truth. She really couldn't hear the crying."

"She couldn't hear the *banshee* because you were the one who had the brush?" I asked trying to understand.

Megan nodded. "I think so. Except I didn't have the brush anymore. I looked for it later and it was gone. I thought Shannon took it so then we argued about that as well. I could tell I hurt her feelings. I don't know why I was so mean to her. It wasn't like me. We never argued."

"Maybe the ghost--the *banshee*--made you act different?"

"That's what I think. Something about the brush made me behave strangely." A thought suddenly occurred to my cousin. She looked at me funny. "But you don't seem any different. I wonder why?"

I thought about it. Did I feel weird? The whole situation was crazy, but I didn't feel any different. "Maybe because I didn't have it as long? It was only like a minute. I brushed my hair and put it back."

Megan bit her lip like she wasn't sure she believed me, but nodded. "I guess. Anyway, we fought and both of us left that evening in tears. The entire time, real quiet, I could hear the crying of the *banshee* somewhere in the distance."

"How long after you picked up the brush did you hear the crying?" I asked. I started to think about how long it had been...only an hour or so, I figured.

Megan thought about it, clearly understanding where I was going with the question. "We played in the woods in the morning and it wasn't until evening that I heard the crying. It wasn't until after dark that...that..."

Megan collapsed onto the bed into tears at the memory. I didn't know what to do. I knew I should comfort her, but she was a girl. One I barely even knew at that. I put my hand on her arm. "It's okay," I mumbled.

After a few minutes, she sniffed and wiped at her eyes. She looked so tired, but also different somehow. Like she wasn't as scared as before. She seemed determined.

"We won't let it happen again," Megan said. "I won't let her get you."

I didn't really understand what she meant at the time. It wasn't until later that night that it became clear. I wish I had known what she was going to do, but if I had, would I have tried to stop her? I liked to think I would have, but I wasn't so sure.

The rest of the day was a blur. Megan and I were quiet, distracted by her story and worrying about the *banshee*. I kept thinking I heard the crying of the Irish ghost, but every time it turned out to be the TV or Mom's tea kettle or the wind blowing outside.

I knew my mom could tell something was wrong. She even asked me point blank, but I shrugged and said I was tired. I wanted to tell her. I thought she could help, but then I felt silly. As the day went on and nothing happened, I started to think Megan had imagined everything or maybe she even made it all up as some sort of terrible joke.

She spent most of the day reading a book, but I noticed she didn't turn the pages very often.

By dinner I was feeling pretty good again. It was obvious that my cousin was still upset by something, but I had decided it was all silly. I knew there were no such things as ghosts and even if there were, they didn't care about silver brushes.

We ate pizza that night. Megan barely touched hers and said almost nothing at all. My parents gave her space. At one point while we were cleaning up, my mom asked me if Megan and I had a fight, but I told her we hadn't. I don't think she believed me, but she let it drop.

Megan didn't want to play any games that night so we all agreed to a movie, but she started yawning soon into it and asked if she could go read in bed for a bit before going to sleep. I didn't think Megan looked tired at all, but I didn't say anything.

I finished the movie with my parents and tried to get them to agree to another one, but Dad had to work in the morning and Mom was tired.

I started to get ready for bed and was brushing my teeth when I first heard it.

It was quiet, like the wind starting to pick up before one of our bad summer thunderstorms. The sound grew louder, but it was impossible to tell exactly from where it came. It had been sunny all day and I didn't think it was supposed to rain overnight. A small voice in my brain started shouting, "Ghost!" I tried to ignore it.

I finished in the bathroom and went into my bedroom and tried to look calm. I didn't want Megan to see that a little bit of wind had scared me. Plus, she was already scared and I figured it was my job to be strong for her. I didn't know what really happened to her friend Shannon, but if Megan thought it was a ghost, I didn't want to make things worse for her.

The room was already dark. Megan must have turned out the lights while I was still in the bathroom. I really wanted to turn them back on, but I didn't want her to think I was afraid of the dark. I hurried to my bed and climbed in under the blankets. I glanced over quickly at her bed, but couldn't make her out in the dark. I thought I heard her breathing, but it was hard to tell over the loud pounding of my heartbeat.

I closed my eyes and tried to force myself to sleep. After a little bit--it might have been minutes or even hours, I couldn't tell--I heard it again.

Ahhhh! Whaaaaa!

It was quiet at first, but grew louder and louder. As the volume increased it got higher in pitch.

Whaaaa! WhooaaaaAAAH!

I tried to ignore it. I hoped I was dreaming. Megan wasn't even moving in her bed. Couldn't she hear it? Was I going crazy?

AhhhHHHHH!

Finally I couldn't take it any longer and I sat up in bed, my hands over my ears.

"Megan," I whispered. "Wake up!"

She didn't move. Suddenly I felt cold all over. Had the *banshee* killed my cousin? Was I in the same room as a dead person?

I slid out of the bed. It was difficult to do since I couldn't use my hands. I still covered my ears with them. At least with my ears covered I couldn't hear the crying. I didn't know if that meant it stopped or I successfully blocked the sound.

I walked the few steps to Megan's bed very slowly. My eyes were used to the dark now and I could see her blankets more clearly. They were twisted and piled up, but as I bent closer, I saw that my cousin wasn't in the bed.

"Megan!" I whispered, but it was obvious my cousin wasn't in the room. My bedroom wasn't very big. There was no place she could hide.

AhhHHHHH! Youuuuuu!

It was the loudest cry yet and it sounded different now. Closer and more real. Before it almost felt like it was coming from inside my head, but now it sounded real and I could tell which direction it came from. The crying came from the back of the house.

My bedroom had a window that looked over our large backyard. I ran to it and pulled the curtains to the side and let the moonlight in. For the middle of the night, it was bright outside. Part of my brain noticed the large, yellow full moon hanging low in the sky.

I couldn't focus on the moon though. I stared at my cousin.

Megan stood in the middle of our yard, just past the picnic table and she faced the large hedge that formed a sort of fence along the back of the property. She stood perfectly still and faced away from me, staring at the bushes.

I undid the lock on the window and slid it open. As soon as the window was open, the crying became so loud I think I shouted in pain.

YOOOUUUUUUUU!!

"Megan!" I shouted her name. I didn't care if I woke up my parents. I wanted them to wake up. I wanted them to help I didn't understand what was happening, but I knew I needed a grown up.

Finally Megan seemed to hear me. She turned her head a little and I could see the side of her face. She was far away and it was pretty dark, but I don't think she was crying. In fact, she appeared braver and stronger than I had ever seen her.

There was a small flash of light near her hand. She raised the silver brush high above her head and the shiny metal caught the moonlight and reflected it. She had it! Did she have it the entire time? Was this all some sort of joke?

When she held the brush up high, the screaming cry grew even louder.

Myyy....BRUSHHH!!

What I saw next will stay in my mind for the rest of my life. When I go to sleep at night I still see it. If I'm in a dark room, I see it. When I stand and look at myself in the mirror, I see it.

Very slowly, a figure emerged through the thick bushes at the back of the property. I knew that was impossible. The bushes were so thick they were almost like a wall. I couldn't squeeze through them even when I was smaller. But this...thing...passed straight through without a problem.

It was very skinny and wearing a long dirty gray dress that flowed along the ground. Her hair hung straight down and stretched past her waist. Her hands reached out in front of her, the fingers were long and almost like a skeleton's except for dirty, broken fingernails at the tips.

But it was the face that I still dream about to this day. It was long and bony with almost no flesh. Once I saw pictures of some prisoners from a war a long time ago. They had been kept in terrible jails and had almost no food to eat. It made their cheekbones stick out and their chins look pointy. The *banshee* was a hundred times worse than that.

Where her eyes should have been were only dark, black pits and her mouth...her mouth was the worst of all. The banshee's jaw hung low, her mouth open wider than should have been possible. I couldn't see any teeth, but I could have sworn that something glowed inside that terrible mouth. A dark bluish-purple light that got brighter and darker as she screamed.

YOOOUUU HAVE MYYY BRUSHHHHH!

The *banshee* was so loud I thought the windows would break. I thought my eardrums would burst. My parents must have heard it. The entire neighborhood must have heard it, but nobody came running. No one was going to help.

"Megan!" I screamed her name.

This time the *banshee* heard me. She started to turn those terrible dark eyes to me. That mouth was going to face me and I knew she would scream and that would be it. If she made that terrible noise directly at me, I knew I couldn't take it.

Right before the *banshee* turned completely toward me, Megan waved the brush again. She yelled something, but I couldn't understand it. I think it was in Gaelic. Whatever she said, it got the *banshee's* attention.

The ghost turned quickly back and moved toward her.

Right before the *banshee* reached her, Megan turned and looked at me. I could tell she was scared, but she smiled. I knew she was doing this for me. Not just for me. For her friend Shannon. She understood what she did.

The *banshee* was right behind her. It wrapped its long arms around my cousin and leaned over her. The long, stringy hair of the ghost fell over the front of my cousin and I couldn't see her anymore.

There was a terrible scream. To this day I couldn't be sure if it came from the *banshee* or Megan. Then the *banshee* slid quickly backwards, dragging my cousin along with her slid through the bushes and disappeared forever.

About the Authors

David Kobb is an author and educator. He lives in northern Indiana with his wife and pet werewolf (that happens to look a lot like a small rabbit). He enjoys hockey, camping with Bigfoot, and is a close friend to all things that go bump in the night.

Shawn Kobb is an author who works as a diplomat on the side. Maybe it is the other way around. He currently lives in Austria with his wife and a dog named Rosie. When not busy trying to scare kids with his over-active imagination, he keeps busy writing books for adults. You can learn more about his other work at shawnkobb.com.